Christine Glover

Edited by Jayne Wolfe

Cover Design by Sweet N' Spicy Designs

# COPYRIGHT

about subsidiary rights contact the author via her website.

www.christineglover.com

ISBN: 978-1543247626

Discover all of Christine's future releases by signing up for her non-spammy newsletter here:

http://eepurl.com/L8Yh5

*Thanks to all my readers, especially my fabulous street team—the Passionettes! You make my world a happier place. XX*

Chapter One

Addison Carrington pulled into Malibu General Hospital's parking lot. She noted the barrage of news crews, tabloid reporters, and photographers crowding around the entrance and groaned. Ryder Bennett's ass wouldn't be easy to save from the publicity of a car crash that killed his Olympic teammate's wife, Tiffany. But then nothing about taking over Ryder's portfolio for her father's PR agency would be simple.

She checked her face in the mirror. The last time she'd seen Ryder, Addison had been an awkward nerd with a weight problem. But today the woman reflected in the small mirror no longer carried extra pounds or bore the imperfections of blemishes.

Ryder could never hurt her again. Though her heart still fluttered uncontrollably at the thought of seeing him. Something she'd successfully avoided for eight years. *Stop it Addison. He's a way to prove to*

*Father you're ready to take over the agency after you fix Ryder's major league screw up.* She'd already arranged for someone to head to his Los Angeles penthouse to pack a suitcase of clothes and other essentials. No way would she let the press get a chance to catch him alone.

Carrington Agency's lawyers had already started negotiations with the District Attorney in charge of the case. Hopefully, they'd avoid a long, drawn out court battle. Deep down, in a place she'd kept closely guarded, Addison didn't believe Ryder would endanger another person's life. Maybe a person's heart, like hers. But not a person's life. Grabbing her designer black briefcase, she opened her car's door and stepped with all the confidence she'd worked to attain toward the crowd milling on either side of the front doors.

Ahead, the sliding glass doors opened to reveal an orderly standing behind a wheelchair with Ryder in it. Her throat tightened. The crash had spared the mountain bike champion major injury, but a small row of stitches crossed the bottom left side of his strong jawline. Still, nothing could detract from his sexy athletic build, which his crisp white dress shirt and torn jeans emphasized to perfection.

Ignoring the flashes of cameras, the questions shouted by the reporters, she squared her shoulders and pushed through the throng toward the one man who held the key to her professional future.

He moved to stand. "Where's your dad?"

"Recuperating from a mild heart attack at our estate in Palm Springs." She placed her hand on his shoulder, stopping him. "Don't move, and keep your mouth shut until we leave." She squeezed his muscles, and forced him to remain seated.

A tic jumped in his temple, and his electric blue eyes locked onto hers. "You sure you can change reality?" Ryder asked. "Tiffany's dead. Eric's quit the cycling team. My coach is threatening to drop me, and the negative publicity is bringing every chick I've dated to the tabloid talk show circuit to grab their fifteen seconds of fame. I don't want to lose my career, but this shit isn't going to be easy to fix."

Though the midday California sun white washed the hospital's facade and heated the concrete she stood on, a sudden rush of cold filled her to the core.

The hairs on the back of her neck raised. She didn't like the starkness in his voice.

"You're our top sports client. This is a setback…"

"A terrible accident that left someone dead isn't a minor setback, Addie."

The use of her former nickname sent a thousand tingles through her skin and warmed her more than she dared to admit. It also resurrected other memories she'd rather not revisit. She pursed her lips and willed her mind to regain control over the current hormonal chorus of whoopees inside her. "I answer to Addison now. I'm the best in my field, and I will fix this situation to our mutual benefit," she said, tightening her grip on his oh-so powerful shoulder. "So be quiet, and let me do all the talking. Got it?"

\*\*\*

"The toxicology report is negative. You didn't have a drop of alcohol in your system." Addison crossed her office's plush carpet and gave Ryder the file that held the police department's accident report. "You like speed, and you've got an Olympic gold record for women revolving in and out of your bedroom. But

Tiffany Langston? She's—was—married to one of your best friends. I don't buy what the press is saying."

Ryder tossed the folder onto Addison's desk, then stared through the glass windows that overlooked the Los Angeles skyline. Haze muted the atmosphere, but the endless modern buildings stood in stark relief against the bright June day. Tunneling his fingers through his hair, he took in the vista of the San Gabriel mountains rising in the distance. Pale brown earth and random tufts of yellow grass and sage created a quilt of land he seriously wished he was racing across right now.

Instead he was in an air-conditioned office trying to figure out how to save his career with the one person he'd never expected to work with again. Addie—correction *Addison*—his former tutor. He'd really liked her spirit and had been drawn to her empathetic nature. Hell, he'd been half in love with her, but too afraid to admit the truth. He'd screwed that up royally. The college girl who had hugged him with enthusiasm when he'd aced his economics final had changed a great deal from that sweet, uber smart, nerd.

Pinching the bridge of his nose, and closing his eyes, Ryder tried damn hard to erase the memory of the last time he'd seen Addison. But even now he could hear the shocked gasp, the whimper of a cry after he'd bullshitted the rest of his team about why he'd been nice to *Fattie Addie*. He'd lied to save face, and had hurt her deeply. Regret couldn't begin to explain the internal punch to the gut he'd absorbed while pretending he didn't care, or that he wasn't attracted to his tutor.

Instead, he'd let his ego drive his mouth and had been a prick of epic proportions toward someone he'd genuinely liked. She'd been cute then, but now? Man, oh man, she was fucking hot. Her power suit accentuated the curves of her hips and slim waist and no amount of layering could hide the swell of her full breasts. Mile high stilettos added to her statuesque height and her once short-cropped hair had grown into long, gorgeous blonde waves, which she tamed into a professional, smart style.

"You're right." Ryder turned away from the view to hold her gaze. "There's more to the story."

She crossed her arms and the fabric of her designer cut jacket stretched tight across her cleavage. "Spit it out." She arched a perfectly shaped brow when she caught his glance drop lower. "We don't have time to waste."

Ryder swallowed hard. "Tiffany had issues. She got drunk at the *Beragio* after Eric went home to check on their boys. Started making plays on the other guys—I got her out before the paparazzi caught her giving lap dances and acting like a stripper."

"Good." Addison dropped her arms to her sides and the tiny line between her eyebrows disappeared. "Witnesses will help corroborate the counterattack I've planned."

"No way." Ryder closed the distance between them to stand toe-to-toe with her. "Eric doesn't need to know about this shit. His sons lost their mother. I won't drag his family through the mud."

"You have an obligation to this agency to maintain your contracts with your sponsors. They're threatening to drop you."

"That's bullshit," Ryder said. "I make one mistake and they want to drop me? I can't lose the sponsorships, or my spot on the Olympic team." Everything he'd worked toward remained in jeopardy, but he didn't want to hurt Eric and his family with the truth.

"Exactly. That's why you have to let me use this information."

Her nostrils flared, and the pulse in the hollow of her throat fluttered wildly. Interesting. More than frost flowed through her veins. "The accident wouldn't have happened if I hadn't insisted on taking her home," Ryder said. "So maybe I am partly to blame."

"You were trying to protect her family from a scandal. Ironic considering you're the one embroiled in a public relations nightmare as a result."

Ryder paused, took in the worry he heard in her voice. And the slight hint of understanding accompanying it. They'd been friends once and he'd discovered that she had an empathetic heart—she deserved to hear the entire truth even if he wouldn't let her use it. He'd hoped she'd see the bigger picture even though she exuded more frost than icebergs floating in the Arctic Ocean.

"I didn't know Tiffany had the hots for me when I pulled her away from one of the other guys." Ryder inhaled a deep breath, and Addison's feminine floral perfume teased his senses. Somewhere beneath the cool professional exterior, he had to believe his Addie still existed. But then, he'd blown their friendship and he couldn't be sure. She was here to do her job. And despite the tell-tale signs of physical attraction, nothing special existed between them anymore. Not after what he'd done. "We were rounding the corner before the turn off to their place in Malibu when she groped me."

Addison nibbled her lower lip, and that tiny line between her brows returned. "Go on."

"I pushed her off, but she got wicked crazy. Tried to grab my dick a second time. When I shook her off, she jerked the steering wheel. I lost control of the car. Now Eric's a widower and his sons don't have a mother."

"You're not to blame for her actions. With witnesses and the toxicology report I can neutralize the negative press within twenty-four hours."

"I won't let them suffer more than they already

have—find another way to save my butt, *Addison*." Ryder shoved his hands into his pockets. He'd made a lot of dumb ass mistakes in his life, including the shit that had landed him years earlier at Saddle Creek Ranch for juvenile delinquents. He'd learned then to live by rules he refused to break, even though one particular rule niggled at the far reaches of his brain, making him cringe inwardly. "You said you were the best. Prove it."

Chapter Two

Addison took in the length of Ryder's muscular body. He'd planted his feet in a wide stance and pushed his broad shoulders back. Regardless of the consequences to his lucrative mountain bike career, he stood solidly, ready to fight her plans. That determination, and cocky athletic arrogance had garnered Ryder dozens of championships, trophies and Olympic gold medals. It had once upon a time been shared with her side-by-side while they studied economics. The word *fail* didn't exist in his vocabulary. Ever.

A knot pulled tight at the base of her head. She had to get him to play it her way or he could lose his sponsorships and the sport he loved. Unfairly. Despite the inadvertent pain he'd caused her years ago, Addison didn't believe he deserved that fate. He cared more about how the details of the accident would impact his former teammate than about himself.

But Addison had to convince Ryder his way was wrong, or her father would never have faith in her ability to run Carrington Agency. And her father had to retire permanently, or risk another heart attack. As hard as it had been to gain his approval throughout her life, Addison loved her father. She didn't want him to die. She wanted to make him proud.

She rubbed the back of her neck, swallowing the fear and frustration scratching her throat. "I admire your desire to protect your friend, but I can't agree with you throwing away your career for him."

"I won't have to throw it away if you're as good as you claim you are," Ryder said, tilting his head to shoot her an I-dare-you look. "Losing my spot on the Olympic team will fuck everything up. That can't happen."

"I'm better than good," she said with feigned nonchalance though her heart pumped at lightning speed behind her sternum. She'd always been a sucker for his teasing, sexy glances. Damn it. "But can you deliver what I want on demand?"

He raked the length of her body, and all the way

back up to lock onto her gaze, attraction gleaming in his pupils. "Never doubt my ability to perform."

Electricity charged between them and the room seemed to shrink. One step closer and she'd evaporate the minute distance between them. Oh, she wanted to bring him to his knees, make him beg for her in ways he'd claimed he never would beg. But she had a job to do. No way would she cross the professional line between them and risk losing the goals she'd worked so hard to attain.

Addison stepped back and rested her hip on her desk, inhaled a deep breath and tried not to think about how Ryder's clean, crisp male scent made her mouth water. After waiting several beats, she picked up the police report. "I don't need to bring more pain to Eric and his family to get you back in the public's good graces," she said, then slid the folder into the bottom of her file trays.

"You promise to keep the information I've shared with you a secret?"

"Yes." Addison nodded, while mentally crossing her fingers and schooling her features into an unreadable mask. "I'm confident you'll live up to my expectations for your public relations' campaign." However, she personally reserved the right to confirm his story behind the scenes if she needed a backup plan. Ryder didn't always know what was best for him. Now she'd make sure she covered his proverbial sexy ass.

"Okay, I trust you." Ryder pulled his hands from his pockets and held one out. "After all, you're the reason I got to stay on the university's cycling team. Shake on it and we have a deal."

Addison hesitated. The last time she'd gotten Ryder out of a shit pile of worry, she'd thought he'd cared a little about her. Not just as a tutor, but as a woman.

Big mistake.

But that naive young woman had grown up and no longer carried a secret crush on Ryder. His motivation to protect his teammate chipped away at her long held belief that he was a self-centered jerk, but she couldn't let emotion guide her choices. She'd control the outcome for their mutual benefit. "Deal," Addison said, placing her palm in his. "But this means you must follow all my instructions without question. Understood?"

She expected Ryder to give her the typical, male version of a chest thumping power grip before releasing her hand. Instead, he gently squeezed longer than a respectable business arrangement handshake required. A tingling sensation, almost a spark of energy, charged through her skin and shot straight through her. His grateful, apologetic look made her pause.

"Understood." He broke their contact and his full lips lifted in a half smile that had probably charmed the panties off dozens of women. "You're the boss. Can't wait to see what you make me do first."

There was a hint of teasing in Ryder. Just as when he'd been freaked about losing his spot on the university's team, now he switched on the guy who acted as if nothing major would annihilate his athletic career. He'd caused many a night of wishful gee-I'd-take-my-panties-off for him thoughts. Hell, once she'd had a journal full of her fantasies. She'd burned the foolishness in a fit of hurt and betrayal.

She wanted to hold onto that hurt, use it to keep her attraction to him at bay. But now she'd gotten a glimpse of the real man behind his charming, devil-may-care mask, and her resolve faltered. That guy had hero stamped all over him, not heartbreaker. And he posed a dangerous threat to her closely guarded heart.

\*\*\*

"Good news," Addison said as she walked into her living room the following Monday morning. "Our lawyers brokered a deal and you won't have to appear in court. Spares us a media circus."

Ryder closed his laptop, and stretched his arms behind his head, peering at her. Online tabloids hadn't backed off slamming him for his role in Tiffany's death. But at least Addison had total control over the legal situation. Plus, she'd made sure he stayed in her sight, and had brought him to her home in Malibu after she'd picked him up at the hospital. "What kind of deal?" he asked, wondering if she owned anything in her closet besides neutral colored power suits and mega high heels. Not that the heels didn't incite all kinds of interesting ideas about her legs wrapping around him while he drove into the hot body he knew existed beneath her business armor. She'd already worked tirelessly for him… would she be the same in bed?

Addison intrigued him. Now he wanted to reconnect with her in ways that had less to do with his physical attraction, and a whole lot to do with his fascination about figuring out what made her tick. He couldn't wait to see what her clever mind had in store for him.

Her brilliant mind and her sexy body hadn't made sleeping down the hall from her throughout the weekend easy. Hell, he figured he had a serious case of deadly sperm build up, too. But their arrangement would remain strictly professional per her orders. Still, he couldn't resist trying to get the fun girl he once knew, albeit a shy one, to emerge from her self-made corporate ice shell.

"One where you're not riding anything other than a bike for three months. Community service, but that'll be good for our publicity campaign. Visits to hospitals, schools, talking about being a responsible driver." Addison ticked her left index finger with her right one while she rattled off the details. "First visit is tomorrow. I'll drive."

He groaned. She might have a vehicle built for speed, but she drove the thing like a granny going on a Sunday church drive. "What about my coach?" She'd even taken over communicating with his team about Ryder's future. He felt like a fucking pussy instead of a man, but he'd do anything to protect the Langston family.

"You're on temporary leave until this fades away. He doesn't want to drag the rest of the team into your mud. However, he expects you to train in the interim." She glanced at him through her lashes. "Your doctors clear you to hit the trails?"

"Yes." He rubbed the skin below his stitches. "No concussion. I've taken harder hits on the race circuit."

"Your next pre-Olympic race is in July." Addison circled the open living room, pausing to stare through the floor to ceiling glass doors that overlooked the Pacific Ocean. "My assistant is finalizing this week's schedule of personal appearances and faxing them to my office here. You'll continue to lay low while I spin the press announcements."

"Yes, boss." He'd agreed to follow her lead, but man, oh man, Ryder had a restless itch to escape, disappear into the Sierra Nevada mountains and hole up in his retreat for fucking ever. "That's all cool, but I can't train if I'm kissing sick kids and talking to high schoolers about the evil consequences of reckless speeding."

Her long sigh echoed in the sparsely decorated room. "Part of the leniency deal means you have to be under my constant supervision. I can't be hauling you from here to the San Gabriel mountains and back while running Carrington Agency."

"Whoa, wait a minute here." Ryder shoved his laptop onto the leather couch, and bolted to his feet. "You're my public relations rep, not my babysitter." If he had to be with Addison twenty-four seven, seven days a week until he returned to his team in July, he'd go nuts. Not because her mausoleum mansion suffocated him from the inside out, but Addison did things to him, made him want in ways he'd never wanted. He wanted to peel those damn suits off her and more. He wanted to find out if the empathetic friend he'd once known still existed beneath all her layers of ice, frost, and professional perfection.

"I don't like this anymore than you do, but I formulated this plan because I knew it would work."

"You think you could have considered consulting me about this brilliant idea before you executed it?" Because the more time he spent alone with Addison, the harder it would be to resist figuring out how to unleash the passion and heart he'd caught glimmers of when she let her guard slip.

Her shoulders stiffened, and she didn't turn away from the view. "I gave you a major concession when I promised to keep your secret, Ryder. You said you trusted me. So trust me about this decision. It's the only way to prove you're reformed. No one would put the two of us together romantically. Ever."

Well, hell. Why did she have to sound so devoid of anything remotely close to human? Especially when there'd been plenty of heat flying between them two days ago? Plus, the coastal highway and beaches in Malibu wouldn't cut it for his brutal, daily regime to prepare for what could possibly be his last Olympic appearance.

Ryder crossed the floor and stood next to

Addison. "I have to train on mountain courses with rugged terrain—the tricks, the jumps and landings that bring me victories require hours of practice," he said. "No way the coach will keep me on the Rio de Janeiro team if I'm not in peak condition. I have to win the race in July. Otherwise, proving to the world I'm a boy scout will be a waste of your time."

"If you'd let me tell the press the truth we wouldn't be in this position," Addison said.

"That's non-negotiable."

"Agreed, but my father's not well enough to run the agency." She glanced his way. "I can't ask him to cut his recuperation short so I can be available for all your training sessions."

He heard the slight catch in her voice, and a sheen of moisture darkened her hazel eyes. Ryder knew she'd never been close to Alexander Carrington, but he was her only parent. If her father died, she'd be alone in the world.

"I'm sorry," he said softly. "I owe him big for getting me to where I am today." And Alexander gave a shit about his daughter even when the guy had no clue about how to communicate with his geeky nerdette. Ryder's folks didn't care about him other than as a commodity for a handout, or a bailout in his father's case. The one good thing that had come out of his twisted family had been getting sent to Saddle Creek Ranch. That, and his kid sister Samantha. She'd ended up on the right side of the law despite the hell they'd grown up in.

"He has to retire if he wants to stay healthy," she said, clasping her hands. "I can't run off to the mountains with you so you can train. What about all the PR ops I've arranged? Crap. Why didn't I think about your training when I agreed to be your guardian?"

"You could telecommute—delegate. It's not like everything is set in stone yet." He'd lost his independence, freedom and he damned well wanted to regain some control over the situation. Another part of him wanted to show Addison she didn't have to be strong all the time. "Reschedule the ops to be in other places besides Los Angeles."

She dropped her arms by her side, then turned to face him. "I'll tell the press what we're doing. Get promo shots of you training—work in the element of how you want to make up for what happened by bringing home the gold again."

The little line between her brows had returned, but Ryder considered that a win. He loved that cute little line. How many times had he observed it when she had leaned over his economics books while explaining the principles in terms he could understand?

Her academic mind quickly processed new approaches to saving his career. So why didn't that seem like enough anymore? Sure, she was professional, but he wished he hadn't fucked up their friendship. He shouldn't expect her to be all warm and fuzzy toward him. He should stay away, let her do her job, but Ryder ignored the internal warning bells and acted on impulse.

He pulled Addison into his arms. "Thanks for hearing me out," he said, then kissed the little line. Because the truth he'd never admitted to anyone years ago had been he'd always wanted to know what it would be like to hold Addison.

Though he wasn't even close to being in her league.

# CHRISTINE GLOVER

Chapter Three

The brief brush of Ryder's mouth against her skin did more to undo her resolve to keep him at arm's length than anything else he could have done. For the first time in the weeks following her father's heart attack, Addison relaxed. Standing in the circle of his warm embrace had her on the brink of wishing he'd bring his lips lower to kiss hers.

Which would be wrong, wrong, wrong. And it could lead to all kinds of complications neither of them could afford, especially her. "I've got to contact my people at the agency, and pull together a new press release." Addison placed her palm on his chest to end his hug. Breaking away from Ryder's heat and masculine scent, she swiveled on her heel and walked toward the hallway that lead to her home office. "Prep me a list of what you need from your penthouse as well as anything you require from your retreat in the Sierra Nevada Mountains."

She had to remain aloof though her knees trembled while she moved away from Ryder's tantalizing presence. And every nerve ending currently fired all kinds of do-me-now messages to long deprived erogenous zones, which made it difficult not to look over her shoulder at him one more time.

*Do not let your body do the talking. And for god's sake, don't ever let him get close again.* Keeping Ryder's portfolio lucrative for the agency mattered. Nothing else. Her rebellious hormones calmed by the time she entered her office. She sank into her chair, grateful for a reprieve from Ryder's overwhelming, masculine pull.

She'd created the space to reflect who she'd always be—a lover of books and cozy reading spaces. Colorful blankets had been tucked into a woven basket next to an oversized, yellow chair with a matching ottoman. A small table housed a reading lamp and her beloved e-reader. Everything had been placed in a corner next to a fireplace that she used whenever the weather allowed.

Addison opened her antique looking desk's drawer, and pulled out her files. Then she buried herself in the tasks she needed to complete before the end of the day. For the next two hours she sent out a flurry of emails to her press contacts, texted her assistant with instructions to expedite Ryder's retreat from Los Angeles, and called her father to touch base.

"How are you doing?" she asked.

"I'd be doing great if I knew the details about Ryder's situation," he griped. "Are you sure you have the campaign under control? Sponsors still on board?"

Addison opened a drawer and pulled out a cough drop, then popped it into her mouth to relieve the tension scratching her throat. "He's cooperating," she said after tucking it into the corner of her cheek, then she gave her father a quick rundown about her media campaign.

"Not sure I agree with the court ordered supervision, but you're not his type and you're too smart to get mixed up with a player like Ryder."

The tension in her throat thickened. "Gee, thanks, Dad," she said and sucked on the drop. "I'll call you after we get settled. Don't worry about anything at the agency. I've got all the bases covered."

"We'll see about that," her father said. "Keep me in the loop. I want to make sure nothing falls through the cracks."

"I will."

And there it was. The total lack of complete trust in her abilities. Sure, they'd gotten closer since she'd remade herself into a perfect size six with flawless skin and hair to complement her dedication to their company, Addison wondered if her father would ever truly approve of her.

Crunching the cough drop and swallowing, she turned her chair around to look at the rows of books lining the cherry shelves. Her childhood favorites— *The Secret Garden, The Wonderful Wizard of Oz* to name a few— and a dozen teenage series books with their well-worn spines had been interspersed with her business texts and financial reports. Here and there one of her go-to romances peeked out, luring her with the same siren call she'd heard on many a lonely night in her college dorm.

Though she hadn't lived like a nun after her hard won beauty makeover, Addison hadn't found anyone who made her chest ache with longing quite like Ryder. She'd gotten over her crush and moved on. What she never expected had been reuniting with the man and discovering he had a heart after all.

\*\*\*

Two hours after he'd held Addison in his arms, Ryder walked to the stainless-steel fridge and opened it. Diet this's and low calorie that's filled the interior. Instant protein shakes lined the inside of the door, and an assortment of pre-cut raw veggies in plastic containers stood in rows. He shut it and shook his head. Not a carb in sight and he needed plenty of them to train for his next race. He'd have to add pasta, bagels, and bread to the list he'd pulled together for her.

Ryder leaned against the granite counter that separated her modern kitchen from the open living area. A bowl of apples and low sugar meal replacement bars rested on it. He'd kill for a burger and fries. Instead, he grabbed an apple and bit into it.

No wonder Addison had such a perfect, sexy

shape. She'd transformed her entire body, and her personality. Her body felt right in his arms, especially when she'd softened and relaxed long enough for him to feel the heat pulsing between them. She wanted him—and for a moment he'd thought about doing more than kissing her forehead. He'd ached to lower his mouth onto hers and kiss her long, hard, and deep.

Then he'd wanted to take that kiss a whole lot further. Unleash the passion flaring underneath her skin, sparking in her eyes when they'd tangled verbally. He wanted to give her a hell of a lot more than a comforting kiss on the forehead.

Great. Now he'd replaced the hole in his stomach with a major rush of blood to his groin, making his jeans tight. And he had no way to release his pent up energy. Normally, he'd take his frustration out on the bike. Riding hard had been how he'd learned to control all of his problems, sexual or otherwise, especially the pain of his upbringing.

He chewed on another bite of apple when his iPhone vibrated in his back pocket. He pulled it out, quickly scanning the text on the screen. His chest hollowed and a sick feeling moved through him as he read the message from one of the few people he'd maintained contact with after he'd left Saddle Creek, Montana.

*It's Rayne, John had a stroke. He's in a coma. It's bad.*

The apple he'd been gnawing on dropped to the pristine granite counter. Rayne had been a regular tagalong at the ranch when he'd been under his mentor John's watch. But a friend, too. They shared the same shit reality of having an alcoholic parent.

John had been the only example Rayne had experienced of how a real man treated others. Ryder shared that bond with her, too. Rarely did she contact him, but then Rayne had been busy getting her veterinarian's license while he'd been chasing thrills.

None of that mattered now. His heart thumped hard against his sternum. *What hospital?* He punched in the question with shaking hands. He couldn't imagine John as anything but larger than life.

*Saddle Creek Mercy General.*

*I'll be out there by the end of the week.*

*You sure you're allowed to travel?*

Crap. His life had been splattered all over the

fucking tabloids and Internet. The accident and Addison's agreement with the lawyers meant he had to get permission to go. Well, he'd be damned if he took no for an answer. He walked toward Addison's office, determined to make her understand he had to go.

The rules of how to be a real man John had hammered into his head raced through his brain. Ryder had become more than a man during the time he'd been placed with John. He'd learned to choose the honorable way to behave, which had gotten him into this current mess.

*I'll figure something out.*

*Okay. The nurse is calling me. TTYL*

Addison might put on a terrific act as an Ice Queen, but deep down his empathetic friend still existed. He counted on her to hear him out and relent.

He burst into her sanctuary, and Addison looked up, her eyes wide. "You make a habit of invading people's privacy?"

"Only when it's important," he said.

"I don't see a list in your hand," she said.

"The list can wait." Ryder closed the distance

between them, noting the difference between this space and the rest of Addison's impersonal mansion. This room reflected everything he remembered about her sweet nature, and the warmth of her heart.

He'd bank on her compassionate side to emerge to he'd make good on his promise to see his mentor one more time. And while he was at it, he'd make good on a rule—a real man never breaks a woman's heart. He'd broken that one long ago when he'd told the guys he'd never be with a chick like *Fattie Addie*.

\*\*\*

"I don't have time to waste, so you better have a damn good reason for not cooperating with me." Addison stayed put and used the desk between them as a barrier. "Especially when I've rearranged my work schedule to suit your training needs."

He scrubbed his fingers through his hair. "I appreciate it. Really. But something's come up that has to take precedence."

"There's nothing more important than saving your career, which has already been made more difficult by your request to protect the Langston family from the truth."

"There's someone I have to see first," Ryder said, his voice breaking. "Before it's too late."

In all the years she'd known Ryder, and after pouring through his files at the agency, she had learned precious little about his background other than he'd grown up on the rough side of Los Angeles. He refused to talk about his parents, and only mentioned his sister on a few occasions. "Is something wrong with Samantha?" Addison asked.

"She's okay. It's… Christ… John Stone. He ran a ranch for troubled youths in Montana. I got sent there when I was sixteen."

Addison lightly stroked her throat. Of all the things she expected to hear, this wasn't it. "You have a juvenile record?" she asked. Another problem to solve, but she could fix it.

"No. Thanks to John, but now he's in a fucking coma." Ryder clasped the edge of her desk. "He made the difference between me having a shit life and the one I have now. I have to see him before he, if he… Christ."

She'd never seen Ryder like this, not even after the accident taking Tiffany's life. "I've scheduled a full PR photo op and media blitz. You've got to train."

"All I'm asking for is one weekend." His Adam's apple bobbed up and down, and a sheen glimmered in his eyes. "Please Addison. Let me go to him. You know what it's like to lose a parent. And to fear for your father's life. What would you have done if you couldn't say goodbye to your mother, or hold your father's hand while he fought to recover in a hospital room?"

Her throat scraped raw. The memory of her strong willed father's heart attack, the sudden panic that she might lose him no matter how hard she begged for his life, struck her at her core. "I understand," she said quietly. "Where is he?"

"Saddle Creek's hospital." He relaxed his hold, and stepped back. "Less than two hours from Billings. I promise I'll follow every order you give me after this detour."

"We'll take the company's private jet. I'll have my personal assistant book a rental for us."

She stood, grabbed her smart phone and texted the instructions immediately while circling around the desk. "We'll leave Friday. That'll give time for photo ops beforehand."

"Thank you."

Addison held his gaze, read the honest relief in his eyes. God. He'd floored her with the love he clearly held for John. Once again putting himself last when he had so much at stake.

Guarding her heart from the man who had broken it was one thing, but that remaining detached and emotionally distance from Ryder proved extremely difficult when his sudden vulnerability exposed a man with the capacity to care... and to care deeply.

## Chapter Four

"You sure you don't want to be alone?" Addison asked Ryder as they stepped into John's private hospital room at Mercy General. She'd never been a fan of hospitals. Though she remembered little about her mother before she'd passed away from complications due to multiple sclerosis, the sights, smells, and sounds of illness always brought a sick feeling to her stomach.

He took her hand. "No. Please stay."

Outside, the sounds of staff being paged over the hospital's intercom while inside the room the ongoing pump of soft drips of intravenous fluids going into John's arm along with his heart monitor's steady beeping permeated the silence.

The boys of Saddle Creek Ranch stood by their mentor all these years later. That spoke a lot about the man currently lying under a white sheet on a bed with both side rails raised. He'd been hooked up to a lot of equipment with wires leading to other machines measuring his brain waves, a finger clip to check his temperature, and an automatic blood pressure cuff.

A middle aged nurse stood next to John's bed marking in his stats. She glanced at Addison and Ryder with compassion, then returned the chart to the foot of the hospital bed. "John's a tough one." She ushered them with a hand wave. "Talk to him and tell him you're here. If you need anything, press the call button." The metallic slide of the room's privacy curtain followed her quick exit.

Ryder rubbed his jaw, the small row of stitches already removed, and moved his hand to the back of his neck. "What do I say to him?" he asked, staring through the window's aluminum blinds.

A small chair had been placed next to the bed, and Addison noted a pair of well-worn cowboy boots tucked under it. How similar to the pair of practical flat shoes placed in her mother's bedroom before death crept in and ended her suffering. Addison's chest ached and she pressed her free palm over it. "Tell him you love him," she said, knowing that begging a dying person to live wouldn't guarantee a damn thing. Nor would whispered deals and prayers in the middle of the night. "Tell him about what's happening in your life now."

"Right," Ryder's voice cracked. "I'm a tabloid pariah, in trouble with my coach, and most likely to lose my entire career. I'm sure he'll want to hear that."

The heart monitor kicked up a notch, and

Addison shot a look at the readout. "I believe you've got his attention," Addison said, then took his hand. "Now let's tell him how we're going to make sure you're a media darling with another Olympic gold medal to hang in your trophy room in August."

"While we're at it, I'll make sure the only reason any of it will happen is 'cause I've got the smartest public relations person saving my ass," Ryder said.

The heart monitor readout skipped a few beats, and Ryder grinned. "I think he likes you."

Tears pricked hot behind her eyes. The once lost boy inside the man seemed to glow through Ryder. Here stood an Olympic champion with a heart of gold so big he'd risk his reputation to protect his friend's family. He'd even temporarily thrown a PR campaign to the curb to visit the man who had been responsible for giving Ryder a reason to choose honor over vice. "Then you had better introduce us properly."

Ryder's grip tightened on hers, and they moved in tandem to stand next to John. One hand still in hers, he covered John's with the other. "I haven't forgotten the rules of a being a real man," he said. "I will make you proud. And this woman standing next to me? She'll make sure I live up to every single thing you taught me."

A slight movement lifted the right corner of John's thin lips, and his gray brow quirked. Her heart caught in her throat. The stroke had stolen John's speech, but Addison sensed his approval and, by the sheen she'd caught glimmering in Ryder's electric blue eyes, Ryder had seen that same tacit approval.

The man standing beside her for the sake of his mentor chipped away at Addison's closely guarded emotions. He was far more dangerous to her heart than the charming champion mountain biker she'd been ruthlessly trying to keep at bay.

\*\*\*

Addison clickety-clicked on her heels while walking beside Ryder. To the west the Beartooth Mountains rose, their jagged rock faces and granite spires a stark contrast in the expansive sky the color of a robin's egg. Man, he'd climbed and ridden the course John had carved out for him more times than he could count.

Beside him, Addison shivered. "It's colder than I expected for June."

The sun's rays didn't counteract the hint of winter cold whistling in the wind, which matched the plank of ice whacking his chest every time Ryder thought about John's prognosis. "This isn't Los Angeles." He whipped off his vintage bomber jacket and put it over her shoulders before she could protest. "Here. You pack anything other than your power suits and ridiculously high heels?"

"I don't have snow bunny gear in my closet. Too busy busting my tail for Carrington Agency to travel other than for work. Most of my clients don't live in small towns stuck in the middle of the mountain." She tripped over a crack in the sidewalk lining Main Street's corridor. "So no, I didn't."

He held Addison steady, but still she wobbled while they made their way through the row of storefronts and planters filled with colorful flowers. Glancing down, he realized one of her heels had snapped off. "You can't keep walking in those shoes," he said.

"I'm perfectly fine."

"No. You're cold, hobbled, and not prepared for this kind of weather." Stifling a grin, he steered her toward the same shop he'd frequented whenever John had taken the boys into town to restock supplies. "You'll find what you need here."

"*Everything But the Mountain*?" she asked, wrinkling her nose. "I don't think so. No. We'll check into the Saddle Creek Inn. I'll change there."

"Come on. Loosen up," Ryder said. "You're in Montana, not your office. You'd be surprised what Lou carries here." If Louise still ran the joint—he hoped so.

"Ryder Wayne Bennett," Louise called while she bustled to the storefront. "I hoped you'd get out here to see John." She enveloped him in her wiry arms.

He inhaled the familiar scent of her homemade brownies and squeezed her right back, holding onto the closest thing he had to a mother figure. "You finish making my favorite?"

"Sure thing." Louise released him, but still held his shoulders to gaze up at him, her braided gray hair sprouting rebellious curls against her lined cheeks. "Bringing them to Herbs Diner later today. You see John?"

"First place I went." He tilted his head toward

Addison. "My PR rep could use some new clothes while she's staying here. And some decent shoes to handle the terrain."

Louise tucked one hand into her jean pocket and gave Ryder an ear cuff with the other. "John taught you how to properly introduce me to your friends. Surely, you haven't forgotten the basic rules of a real man since you high tailed it out of here and became a famous bike champion."

"Rules? What rules?" Addison asked, her gaze ping ponging between Ryder and Louise.

"Rules of a Real Man." Ryder rubbed his ear, thought about all the other lessons he'd learned from his mentor. And the one epic failure. "I haven't forgotten. Louise. This is Addison Carrington. She's handling my PR makeover and in charge of making sure I don't mess up before the next Olympic trials."

"Pleasure to meet you." Louise held out her hand and gripped Addison's, her eyes measuring Addison from the top of her perfectly styled blonde hair to the bottom of her ill-fated shoes. "You're in luck. I don't sell many size four jeans here, but I've got a pair that will fit you. We got a new shipment of sneakers yesterday. Those should do just fine."

A size freaking four? What did she live on? Yeah—her fridge had revealed her crap diet plan with its rabbit food and low calorie protein shakes. "She'll need bike gear, too."

Addison's mouth dropped, then she snapped it shut. "I—no—no I don't ride."

"You will while you're here." Ryder craned his neck toward the back of the store. "You still rent bikes?"

"Nothing that'll compete with your fancy handcrafted pro circuit racer, but if you're willing to slum it, I can hook you up."

"They were good enough for me when I first started training," he said, then kissed her cheek. "We're bunking at the Saddle Creek Inn for the weekend. I'll grab them before we head out to the course John built."

Louise placed her palm over his hand. "He'd be pleased about you using the course, Ryder."

His throat tightened, and he swallowed hard. "Thanks, Lou. Now let's hook my girl up before she breaks another one of her expensive shoes." And get her away from him before he completely lost it in front of Addison.

## Chapter Five

After Ryder and Addison left the shop, they checked into Saddle Creek Inn. Once there, they dumped her shopping bag along with their luggage in their adjoining rooms. Then they drove to the outskirts of town to bring him to Herbs Diner where he met with some of the former alumni of Saddle Creek Ranch.

Wearing her new jeans, and feeling about ten feet shorter, Addison hesitated by the diner's glass door. "These are your friends. You don't need me tagging along for this reunion," she said, clutching her purse.

She was out of her element, remembering her last encounter with Ryder and his teammates. That hadn't gone well at all. However, it had been the catalyst fueling her complete physical makeover.

Ryder glanced at her fisted hand, then into her

eyes. "You're in my life now, and this week you've already managed to spin the tabloids and media in my favor with your PR campaign." He intertwined his fingers through her free ones. "I want these guys to meet you. It's important to me."

Zings of electricity pulsed through her skin, and desire unfurled low in her belly. Her death grip on her oversized handbag eased and a sultry sensation floated through her. So not good. Yet Ryder's words meant more to her than she could admit. She'd always been a bit of an outsider, and her co-workers didn't cross the tough border she'd created as a mechanism to protect herself.

She should say no to Ryder. But she couldn't resist learning more about him. Not only that, but his gaze mesmerized her.

"Okay, I'll come in to say hi, but then I should head back to the inn and buckle down. From the way my phone's been buzzing, I'm sure I've got a zillion emails to dispatch before the end of the business day in LA."

"Park the iPhone, and give yourself a break." He pushed open the diner's door, a bell tinkled, and they stepped inside. "We're staying long enough to eat dinner and catch up with the guys."

She glanced at the chalkboard with flowers drawn around it in different colored chalk pens. The owner had paired the regular diner fare with some interesting additions of turkey chili, meatballs, rustic salmon, and tofu surprise. They moved between the diner's counter and booths. The healthier selections would allow her to stick to her diet, but her long-lost inner junk food addict screamed for burgers and fries.

Maintaining her self-control wouldn't be easy, but she couldn't back out now that Ryder had reached the booth where two men—both awesome specimens of the male species—quickly stood to make room for her and Ryder. Within moments she'd been introduced to Walker Hammond and Stefano Mercado, along with his traveling companion, Roxie Sullivan.

"How're things in the auto world?" Ryder asked, then lifted a french fry from Stefano's plate and bit into it.

"Hey, get your own food," Stefano protested.

"Can't complain," Walker said. "But I'm

looking to make a big change if things go the way I want." He shot a look over to the counter where a dark haired woman hustled behind it.

"I didn't know Savannah worked here," Ryder said.

"She owns the joint," Stefano said, then shifted closer to Roxie. "Best coffee in town and her cook makes a mean monster cheeseburger when he shows up."

Addison looked at their half-empty platters. The scent of frying onions, burgers and her former favorite go-to comfort food, french fries, filled the air. It had been ages since she'd let an unhealthy carb or greasy burger pass between her lips. Her stomach grumbled, and she grabbed the laminate menu tucked between the napkin holder and a little white vase holding wildflowers to scan it for additional healthy options.

She would not cave to the hunger churning in her belly. No way. And certainly not in front of Ryder.

His leg pressed against hers and a delicious shiver trembled through her, making her crave so much more than the contraband monster cheeseburger on the menu. As much as she wanted to make Ryder her main course, she'd put a clamp on that desire, too.

"I'll have the chef salad with grilled chicken, red wine vinaigrette on the side," she said when Savannah came over to ask for her order with a sunny smile on her face. One definitely not directed at Walker.

Ryder ordered what she had denied herself and then went back to reminiscing with his friends about their days at Saddle Creek Ranch. Whatever wrongs they had committed to be sent to the ranch for remediation, each of the men had long ago shed their backgrounds to become successful in their own rights. An incredible testimony to their mentor's no-nonsense influence over their lives.

While she couldn't erase what had happened as a result of the crash, Addison believed she owed it to the man she'd visited to make sure Ryder's future didn't get screwed up. John had instilled honor and integrity in Ryder. Those qualities drove Ryder to do the right thing for Eric at great expense to himself.

She'd follow up with Eric Langston when they returned to Los Angeles. Discreetly. There had to be some way to give everyone what they needed to move on with their lives, including Ryder's former teammate. Her promise niggled at her, and a smidgen of guilt threatened, but she pushed it aside.

Repairing this particular client's reputation took precedence no matter what.

Their plates arrived and Walker took off to check on Savannah. Addison resolutely took her first bite of the freshly prepared salad. Chewing slowly, she reached for her glass of water and sipped afterward. *Slow and steady. Don't cave to the craving. Don't. Don't. Don't.* But oh, the damn burger smelled like heaven.

Her stomach rumbled.

"You sure you don't want at least one fry?" Ryder said, holding one up and dancing it in front of her face. "Used to be your favorite."

Addison's cheeks heated and she quickly jammed her fork into the chicken strip. "Not anymore," she said primly while delicately cutting the strip into tiny pieces.

"You know you want to," Ryder teased.

"Yeah," Stefano said, smiling. "What's the big

deal? You're so skinny you can eat whatever you want."

"Come on," Ryder said. "Live a little, Addie, and cut yourself some slack. One fry isn't going to hurt you."

Addison hated the teasing in their voices. Though she knew Stefano had no idea that her weight was an ongoing battle, Ryder did. Suddenly, her nose itched and tears pricked behind her eyes. Hot, ugly, wet ones were threatening to burst through the mental dam she'd elevated years ago. "Maybe not." She dropped her fork and pushed his hip with hers to force him out of the booth. Standing, she glared at him. "But shallow, mean words can cause a lot of damage. Fortunately, I repaired the worst of it and I'm better off. So park your fries up your ass. I'm out of here."

\*\*\*

"Crap, I royally fucked up," Ryder said, scrubbing his hand over his face and tunneling his fingers through his hair while Addison rushed to the diner's door.

"What the hell's wrong with sharing a fry?" Stefano asked.

"Everything if it reminds her about the dumb ass

shit she overheard eight years ago." Ryder couldn't believe he'd hurt her when he'd only wanted to get Addison to loosen up, relax with him like they used to do during their study sessions. "I didn't stand up for her then—didn't chase her down to apologize. I'm not repeating that fucking mistake."

"You broke one of John's rules," Stefano said. "I know what that can do to screw up a relationship."

"We're not in a relationship. She's my PR rep, but I have to make up for being a jerk." Not just for how he screwed up today, but for the heartbreak he'd heard in her shocked gasp back then. He'd let foolish male pride drive his actions and words. And though he'd never used the term *Fattie Addie*, he hadn't stood up for her, either.

He glanced at the platters, then moved to pull his wallet out to pay his portion of the bill. "Will twenty cover our meal?"

Stefano shook his head. "I've got this. Go after her."

"Thanks."

He bolted for the diner's exit, stepped outside, and his gaze landed on Addison's ramrod straight stiff back as she approached the SUV. "Stupid. Stupid. Stupid. Why did I let him talk me into going to the diner? He has no idea, none, about who I am and what I want," she said, talking to herself.

His chest tightened. Hearing the tears in her voice, and false bravado filled him with a major case of self-hate. If he could turn back time and replay the entire episode, he'd do it in an instant. "Addison, wait," he called, running toward her. He couldn't do a retake on the past, but he sure as hell could forge a different ending to this situation. One that would prove to Addison she mattered more than he'd ever dared to admit all those years ago.

She glanced at him over her shoulder. "Get a lift from one of your friends after you finish your monster burger." Her eyes glimmered, and her chin trembled despite the firm commanding tone in her voice. "I've got a mountain of files to go over when I get back to the Inn." Addison looked away, digging into her purse until she retrieved the SUV's keys with shaking fingers.

"Addison." Ryder touched her shoulder. "You're too upset to drive, let alone work."

She pressed her forehead on the door panel. "You don't have to be my hero, Ryder. Not like you tried to be with Tiffany." Addison gave a heavy sigh. "I'm angry, but I'm not drunk. I have to get out of here before…"

His throat felt raw. "You aren't angry, you're hurt." He couldn't let her go. "I'm responsible for it. And I'm so sorry. So damn sorry I didn't stand up for you after the guys razzed me about our relationship."

Big plops of water landed on the curb beside the SUV. "I thought you were my friend."

"I was."

She swiped her face. "You sure didn't act like one."

"I was an idiot of epic proportions." He closed the distance between them, and gently turned her to face him. God, it killed him to see the tears tracking down her cheeks. He'd put them there twice in his lifetime and he wanted to replace them with the sunny smiles she'd always had for him before he fucked things up with his tough guy act. "You helped me so much, Addison. I've had the career of a lifetime because of you. Do you have any idea how much that means to me?"

"I was your tutor. Nothing more." Addison gulped in air, but still the tears ran down her face. "It's just that I—I had fun and I mixed up the way we joked around. I made it more in my head. Stupid."

"You're one of the smartest people I know." He brushed away her tears, and held her eyes with his. "You were right, Addison. I liked you. A lot. You made me laugh. You made me believe I could ace the economics final. I loved spending every minute with you. I miss that girl. More than you can possibly imagine."

She blinked. "I was *Fattie Addie*. Remember? No one wanted me."

"Sweetheart. You're wrong," he said. "I wanted you. But you were my agent's daughter. Rich. Smart. Talented. Way out of my league and totally off limits."

"Out of your league?" she asked, sniffing hard. "I was a fat, ugly nobody. And losing fifty pounds hasn't changed who I am on the inside. I'm always one slip away from losing control... food used to be my emotional comfort zone. I can't let it become a crutch for me. I won't."

"I shouldn't have teased you with the french fry," Ryder said.

"Not going to lie." She dropped her gaze. "I wanted it. And the monster cheeseburger. But I know what will happen if I indulge my craving. One bite, one taste, won't ever be enough. And I'll become that loser. *Fattie Addie*."

Her voice sounded small, vulnerable, raw. The pain behind his sternum intensified. He'd never seen her as that girl, but he'd let peer pressure stop him from standing up for her when she needed it most. "You weren't a loser," he said, tilting her chin up. She looked adorable with her tear stained face and the tiny hint of pink at the tip of her nose. "But I get what you mean about what will happen if you indulge in your craving. I want you. In a bad, bad way, Addison. But I'm afraid one bite, one taste won't satisfy my craving."

The pulse in the hollow of her throat fluttered wildly and her hazel eyes darkened. "You want me now because I've changed my physical appearance," she said. "I won't be an embarrassment to be seen with in public."

"You're hot. Sexy. Beyond attractive. No denying how much you turn me on. But that's not why I want to be with you." Ryder touched her forehead with his and caressed her cheeks. "I want you because you're still the same person on the inside. You're someone who cares deeply. You've always given 200 percent to support others no matter how tough the challenge, especially when the challenge is me."

Ryder stroked his thumb over her full lower lip as she trembled in his arms and her breathing accelerated. He couldn't resist the temptation of taking one small taste if only to show her how desirable she was inside and out. He lowered his mouth to hers, intending to give her a simple brush across the lips. One that danced on the edge of friendship, and skimmed around the border of his desire and stopped short of leading to more than they could handle. But when they connected, she felt so right and sweet in his arms that all of his good intentions shot into the stratosphere and flew over the Montana mountain range.

\*\*\*

Addison tried to remind herself Ryder was off-limits, but her body refused to listen. After all, he'd once been her top fantasy man, and being with him during this past week had reawakened her long ago desire. But right now, he'd done more than recharge her rebellious hormones. Ryder had amped the charge of attraction way up with his gentle, tender confession. That endeared him to her far more than the way his clean masculine aroma swirled through her senses, intoxicating her. The softness of his mouth against hers, tentatively tasting along with the emotions he'd stirred, unraveled her ability to think clearly.

Hungry for more than a chaste kiss, Addison tilted her face to give him better access to her mouth. She coiled her arms around his neck, then opened her lips to let his tongue steal inside. She stroked over it, and he licked hers back, deepening their kiss.

Over and over, their tongues danced with each other. Tasting, teasing, and sliding together with sweet exploration, discovering each other and wanting more. So much more. Her hands tangled in his hair, and he clasped her waist, drawing her closer.

Addison clung to him, losing herself in the mesmerizing connection of their mouths melding and becoming one.

Pleasure shot through her nerves until her body ached with hot need. For him. Only him. Her nipples pebbled, sending tingles to her core. Exquisite vibrations pulsed between her legs at the apex of her sex. She had never craved anything, anyone, as much as she craved Ryder.

The buzzing in her back pocket broke through the blood racing through her veins. Suddenly, she remembered where they were and what she'd signed on to do for him. Kissing him, and being kissed senseless had not been part of the bargain when she'd taken on Ryder's PR campaign.

She wrenched her mouth from his, breathless. "We can't do this." Addison placed her palm on his chest to stop him. "Not now. Not when there's so much at stake."

He stepped back, dropping his hands to his sides, his eyes still searing hers with the heat they had ignited. "You're right," he said gruffly. "God forbid the press catch us doing anything."

She shifted her gaze from his, and withdrew her phone to read the message. "Making Miracles Happen has a little boy with cancer who wants to meet his favorite Olympic star next Tuesday," Addison said, slipping straight back into business mode. "That'll be an excellent photo op."

As much as she wanted him, Addison had to remember Ryder was her client. More than that, her father counted on her to show the world this man had reformed his wild, womanizing ways. She could not be one of his conquests. Well, she'd denied herself plenty of temptations during the last eight years.

Ryder would be one more indulgence she'd avoid.

## Chapter Six

Saying no to a french fry, or a humongous bite of a monster cheeseburger, didn't compare to denying herself Ryder, especially when Addison had a first class view of his extremely fine ass. Skin tight bicycle shorts hugged his chiseled butt to perfection while he climbed the mountain trail in his rental bike ahead of her. Addison mentally fanned herself.

"Won't be long until we reach the lake," Ryder called. "We'll break to eat there, then head back."

After getting up at the crack of o'dark early so she and Ryder could pick up their rental mountain bikes, they loaded them for their trek into the wilderness. Now she had an appetite all right.

For Ryder.

Not for the protein bars and water they'd tucked into their small back packs for the hour long bike trip.

"Sounds great," she huffed, and continued navigating her way through the forest trail.

Ugh. Her legs burned with exertion. Sure, she worked out. In a controlled environment offering regular fitness classes along with a yoga program taught by a kick butt instructor who at fifty-five had the physique of a woman half her age. Riding this trail was tougher than she'd expected—not just physically, but emotionally. He'd done more than turn her on last night, he'd touched her heart. That made her want to be with him even more.

"Wait until you see the view," Ryder said, slowing his pace to accommodate hers.

Her bike's wide, powerful wheels crunched over pine needles, broken branches, and rocks. Sunshine landed on the stands of purple wildflowers throughout the trees' bases. She inhaled the sweetness of the blooms along with the earthy scent of moss and vegetation, then pedaled harder.

"How much longer?"

"Less than a mile now."

Today's ride came close to kicking her butt, but nothing compared to the challenge of pretending she wasn't hyper aware of Ryder's incredible, athletic body as they rode through the mature forest. Or the way her heart had become vulnerable to the genuine compassion in Ryder's.

Still, she should never have kissed him back.

Gargantuan mistake.

Because nothing. Not even hours of time logged on her laptop and juggling media requests for Ryder's personal appearances could erase the memory of his tenderness, compassion, and affection. Nor could she forget how his touch sent heat through her entire body.

The taste of him still lingered at the tip of her tongue. Hot, delicious, and all male. It crept into her dreams, and teased her with the promise of his possession. Now she couldn't stop fantasizing about acting on the attraction, or the unspoken emotions, swirling between them. Wind whistled through the evergreen trees swaying on either side of the narrow trail. But the chill it carried from the snow encrusted peaks in the distance had zero impact on the fire flaring through her veins. That he'd backed away without pushing for more spoke volumes about him.

But a tiny, naughty part of her wished Ryder had lived up to his bad boy reputation. Because right now she truly wanted to be a bad, bad girl.

Ahead of her, Ryder followed the left edge of the trail and she kept up, then gasped when their destination came into view. "You rode here every day? Trained?" she asked, awed by the expanse of the ultramarine lake and the surrounding verdant meadows with their pops of colorful flowers.

"Yes." Ryder braked and eased one clipped foot out of the pedal, then braced the bike with his thighs. "John widened the trail, and we added the drops I used for practice before I got picked up by the university's team."

"It's like a postcard." Addison tried to stop next to him, but the forest's wet leaves made her tires slide and she slipped into his side, nearly toppling them over. "Sorry. Looks like I'll never get rid of my inner klutz."

He wrapped his arm around her, then righted her and the bike. "I've seen a ton of pro bikers wipe out here, myself included," he said, still holding her waist.

His hand seemed to sear her, brand her as his. A sudden flush spread from her center outward and a shudder trembled through her. Addison tried to remind herself that Ryder had reacted like any other guy. But her body refused to hear her strict stay-in-control command. And how could she blame it? Ryder's touch felt so damned good.

Out here, in the wilderness, without the pressure to spin his career back into PR heaven, Addison wondered how bad acting on her desire would be. She'd finally put the fantasies she'd spun about him to rest, especially when she knew Ryder had a genuinely good soul. One she yearned to connect with even though she couldn't rely on it to last forever. Not with his career and future at stake. But afterward, she'd have a precious, amazing secret which made the idea of testing Ryder's admission about wanting her *that way* more tantalizing.

***

Addison leaned against Ryder, the metal of their bikes clanging and echoing in the vast empty space, and rested her head on his shoulder. "Thank you for bringing me here," she said.

Holding Addison, Ryder could stay in this spot and overlook the vista of the lake, surrounding meadows, and the snow capped mountain peaks in the distance for an eternity. "Worth the ride, right?" he asked, then tightened his hold and pulled her a little closer. She smelled good, her unique floral scent mingling perfectly with the tang of pine needles and sunshine that haloed around them.

"Absolutely." She snaked her arm around his waist, and ran her palm over his torso. "You bring all your dates here when you were living in Saddle Creek?"

Her voice had a husky tone, seductive as sin, and a zing of electricity charged into his groin, making his cock twitch. If he were reading the signals right, Addison had done an about face on her do-not-touch-me edict. "Nope. You're it," he said after he doused his lust with a huge dose of ice.

Ryder had never brought another woman to his practice trail. But he'd wanted to share this place with Addison. And, if he was honest with himself, he'd thought about it long ago when they'd bent their heads over his reams of study sheets. The urge to connect with her at a visceral, trusting level of friendship resurrected from the minute he'd seen her walking across the hospital's parking lot a week ago.

"Figured bringing you here might help you with your PR campaign," he said. "You could use my background to show the public how I overcame all the odds blah blah blah…you're the genius. I trust you to take what you learn about me and use it well."

He'd become a man here, and had learned lessons to last a lifetime. If anyone deserved to know the real Ryder and where he came from—at least this part of his life—it was Addison. She'd never treated him like a spoiled athlete when she'd tutored him. She'd never made him feel like a jock without brains when he had trouble understanding economics concepts. She'd never asked anything of him other than to be her friend.

"Good idea."

Today he'd be that friend. One she could rely on, especially after what she'd revealed to him last night. After their emotionally charged moment, while she'd been hiding in her adjacent room at the Inn, Ryder had called in a lot of favors to make today's trail ride mean a lot more than a push against nature.

He hadn't brought Addison to the lakeside to seduce her, but... her hand continued to trace circles up and down the side of his torso. Holy. Fuck. All.

"You think you can ride another quarter mile?" he asked through a constricted throat while pointing toward the canvas gazebo he'd arranged to have erected. "I ordered in lunch."

She lifted her head, and her hand stopped torturing him with its sexy touches. "I don't understand. How on earth did you make this happen all the way out in the middle of nowhere?"

He shot her a look through his wraparound sunglasses, grateful for their cover because he doubted he could hide the heat she'd ignited. "You have your ways of getting things done, I have mine." Money, connections, and his sister Samantha's helicopter pilot's license had been weapons in his arsenal to make things right between him and Addison. He shot her his best commercial stock grin. "You still want protein bars and water, or will you let me make up for not feeding you properly last night?"

"Define properly."

"The best clean eating restaurant in Los Angeles catered the meal."

Addison touched his face, then drew it toward her. She brushed her mouth over his—a brief, soft sensation until the tip of her tongue licked his lower lip.

"Then I'm all in," she said when she pulled away and spoke in a slow, sensual, and beyond sexy tone before pushing off and riding ahead of him.

He remained rooted where they'd stopped, unable to take his eyes off her while trying to control the fire pulsing throughout his veins, and thundering in his ears. His lips tingled, and his cock had a life of its own as it strained against the fabric of his shorts.

No way could he ride in this condition—he channeled every mental way he had to kill his hard-on, but hell. How could he kill it when his sex-starved brain couldn't stop zoning in on her sweet, round behind and those long, luscious legs? She was hot in her skin tight spandex bike shorts, and figure hugging jersey. Plus, she was fun, unreserved, and playful. He liked her playful, flirtatious side a lot. Maybe too much.

Something had shifted between last night's all-business no-way-would-she-act-on-it attraction to Addison's sexy, come-on-to-him temptation today. He didn't know why, but right now? Ryder didn't dare analyze the situation. Not when his entire body, brain, and heart had unified into following up on that challenge.

Chapter Seven

"Don't worry," Addison said when Ryder finally arrived at the picnic site he'd conjured into being with a flick of his mogul wand. "I won't let it out that I whupped America's Olympic Gold champion in a mountain bike contest." She'd pulled off her helmet and removed her cycling shoes before lounging on the luxurious blankets and pillows.

"Wouldn't be good for our PR campaign." Ryder took his time dismounting his bike, leaned it on one of the gazebo's poles, and then moved into the shelter of the brightly colored canvas. "You check out the basket?"

Her breath caught in her throat. Dear Lord, watching Ryder was like watching perfection in fluid motion. His body also came with a super, amazing, guaranteed-to-please with a sticker on it loving—

based on the size of his bulge.

A thrill traveled to her core, warming her from the inside out. That she could cause that kind of reaction in Ryder brought a rich, decadent satisfaction that tasted way, way better than the most sinful dessert she'd ever eaten. Sure, self-discipline had its place—at the dining room table—but this was different. Ryder had reached a place in her heart few people, maybe none, had ever seen. Now her heart warred with self-discipline in a big way.

"Yes." She pointed to the open lid and the plates she'd already arranged on the red and white striped blanket along with the requisite cutlery to manage eating the delicious meal he'd had flown in. "This looks great—my favorite restaurant's dishes. How'd you find out about it?"

He finished taking off his equipment, then lowered himself to the blanket beside her. "Your assistant gave me the name, and the chef pulled together the menu." Ryder plucked out a container and opened it to reveal a fragrant mélange of mixed fruits lightly glazed with a beyond amazing balsamic vinaigrette.

Warmth filled her. Ryder had gone to all this trouble and her heart beat faster than she'd ever imagined possible. His scent, all masculine and woodsy, along with the palpable electricity arcing between them amped up the wow factor even more. But Ryder appealed even more because he'd focused his energy on showing her he cared. Her feelings mattered.

Her tummy grumbled, and she flushed. "We better dig in," she said, unable to take her eyes off the sinew of his forearms and the fine dark hairs she hoped to discover in other, wonderful places on his body.

"Absolutely." Ryder pulled out the rest of the picnic's containers and locked his gaze onto hers. "I'm starving."

His shades no longer hid his eyes, and their brilliant blue color had darkened. Mesmerized, she licked her lips. "And I'm famished," Addison said. First, she'd dig into the delicious food, then she'd dig into the man who had provided it. No way would she let this opportunity to have what she had always wanted slip from her fingers. But could she have him, then let him go when her emotions were all tangled up with her physical yearning?

Half an hour later, with the sounds of leaves rustling and birds trilling while they flitted from wildflowers to the branches in the trees in the forest bordering the meadow, Addison finished her last sumptuous bite of the good-for-her lunch. "Chef Stacey outdid herself," she said. "So yummy."

They'd chatted about everything and nothing while enjoying the meal. Their former camaraderie had returned, and Addison sincerely hoped that no matter what happened after this afternoon, they'd remain friends.

"You want to head back?"

"No. Not really." She stretched her legs out, brushing his thigh. "Sun's still out, and why rush when we have the entire meadow to ourselves?"

"True," Ryder said. "No one's within miles."

How incredibly romantic would it be to lie beneath the shelter of the gazebo with Ryder? The sweet aroma of long grass, wildflowers, and clean Montana air mingling with theirs? She wanted, oh how she wanted to pretend this bubble could exist forever.

He'd never make the first move. Not when she'd denied him yesterday. Addison had to cross the divide she'd erected between them.

She placed her hand on his, and looked at his profile. How many times had she mentally traced the line of his high brow all the way to his strong jawline? How many times had she fantasized about tunneling her fingers through his dark, unruly hair? How many times had she wanted, yearned, desired to feel his skin slide against hers while they made wild, crazy love?

How many times had she wanted to carry that love in her heart and know that it was equally returned?

Too many.

But she'd let this fantasy to come to life here, in the safety and privacy of their hidden meadow. Where she'd be in control. Period. Because no way would she risk her heart and her future for him. Taking in a deep breath of mountain air to fortify herself, Addison shifted closer to Ryder.

She brushed her lips onto his cheek and then

tasted his spicy skin with her tongue. "I'm still hungry for more," Addison said.

***

Ryder's ears thundered and his blood ran hot through his veins all the way to his groin. Holy. Fuck. Yes. He sure as hell was hungry for more, but somehow he forced his sex fogged brain cells to operate. "I didn't plan this picnic to convince you to have sex with me," he said. "You said no. I get why. We're in a professional relationship." But man, oh fucking man, he wanted to act on the fire Addison had ignited.

"Exactly," she said, licking and nibbling her way to his mouth and then rolling over to straddle him. "And this can't happen again. Not when we get back to reality. But now? In this gorgeous mountain meadow in the middle of Montana? Where gourmet meals are flown in on a whim? This isn't reality." Her teeth playfully dragged his lower lip into a kiss.

His cock hardened to granite. No denying the heat and moisture and the sweet scent of Addison's arousal. He wanted her. She wanted him. But would once be enough? He'd have to take the chance because saying *no* wasn't an option. Not only for the real, physical need burning between them, but he couldn't lie and reject Addison. As bold as she acted, he'd held her in his arms when she'd been at her most vulnerable and bared her soul to him. He wouldn't hurt her even it meant fucking up his own mixed up heart.

"You're right. This isn't reality," he said. This was heaven and he'd lose himself in the moment even if it killed him later.

"You always were a quick study," Addison said, then deepened her kiss, sliding her tongue into his mouth.

Ryder stroked over it and she moaned, writhing her gorgeous ass on his groin. Their kiss spiraled hotter, faster, more demanding while he pulled her even closer and answered her demand for more. Taking. Giving. Taking again.

She tasted like berries and the wildflowers scenting the light mountain breeze. Now that he could savor her mouth, his entire body was greedy for the rest. His heart even more. "Addison," he said, cupping her bottom and rolling them until he hovered over her. "You're so sweet. So, so sweet."

"I don't want to be sweet." She arched her back and pressed her full breasts against his chest. "I want to be bad. Really, really bad."

"Then you're in luck because I'm the poster boy for bad."

Ryder melded his lips onto hers, and kissed her while he roamed his hands over her curves, her soft sighs and moans vibrating into him so deep he nearly lost all control. He slipped his palms under her shirt and hers skimmed beneath his jersey, then traced her way along his back. Their motions matched each other, equals freely exploring each other.

"Ryder," she said, her voice ragged, raising her hips to meet his. "More. I want more."

Shudders of pleasure coursed through him, and his cock throbbed with the rush of blood filling it. "That makes two of us."

Suddenly, slow discovery transformed to fast, frenzied demanding removal of the barriers of their clothing until they were pressed, skin to skin, body to body, sliding together—hot and wet and slick with need. Their breathing rushed in and out, edging them higher and higher to the point of no return.

Desperation to plunge into her, mindless and lost to the sensations building in him, warred with his desire to please, and take her over the abyss first. Pleasing her won, barely. But he had to show her with his body what his mind still struggled to comprehend.

He cared.

Regardless of what happened after today, Ryder wanted Addison to believe she was worthy of love. He wanted her to feel adored. He wanted her to forget he'd ever broken her heart. Ryder wanted to be the man who gave her the power to demand she be cherished for the rest of her life even if he would never be the right guy for her.

Emotions tangled in his brain, made him want to spill the feelings stirring inside him for Addison, but he blocked the desire by lowering his lips to her breasts and taking one into his mouth. Her hands raked across his shoulders and she arched closer to him.

Ryder swirled his tongue over her taut, rosy colored nipples and she gasped, her hips wildly moving beneath his. He pinned her with his body, ignored the hot need vibrating deep in his shaft, and continued savoring her breasts one at a time, sucking her in harder until she moaned his name over and over in raw, ragged breaths.

"You're so close, Addison. Let yourself go— come for me."

"I can't ... it's too much."

"I've got you," Ryder said, then sucked her sweet nipple into his mouth and nipped the sensitive flesh while tracing his hand down the slope of her slim waist until he reached the soft curls covering her slick sex. "Hang onto me, sweetheart. I'll take you where you want to go."

"Oh. I—Ryder..." she threaded her fingers through his hair, and held him to her sexy, responsive breasts. "Now. Touch me now."

His heartbeat pounded in his ears and his cock seemed ready to explode, but this was about Addison. He'd give her what her body craved first. Ryder stroked the seam of her sex, parting the flesh until he found the pulsating bundle of nerves at the apex. "Is this what you want?" he asked, looking up from her breast to take in her flushed cheeks and the passion glazing her eyes.

"Yes. Oh, yes."

He slipped his finger into her, then swept her slick arousal over her clit. It jumped at his touch, and shudders waved through her entire body. Oh yeah, she was so damned close to shattering beneath him. "I want you to come for me, then I'm going to make you come all over when I'm inside you." Ryder moved his cock across her hips to let her feel how he bordered the line between control and losing it completely.

She moaned, trembled and arched her back, her release shuddering through her and spasming against his hand. He held her until she went limp and soft and pliant in his arms. Raising up on one elbow, Ryder gazed at Addison's pretty flushed cheeks and her sweet lips.

"You're amazing." He kissed her closed eyelids and brushed her damp hair from her temples. "Never doubt that, Addison."

Her gorgeous hazel eyes fluttered open and locked onto his. "You're not at all what I expected," she said while spreading her legs languidly to cradle his groin.

"What did you expect?" he asked, then pressed

his forehead onto hers, not daring to admit what thrummed through his sex fevered mind. *Like me. Love me. Let me be the guy who'll protect you and love you forever.*

He'd promised her *for now.* Asking for more couldn't be part of the equation.

\*\*\*

Tender. Ryder had been tender when Addison had expected crazy, insane sex and nothing more. Tiny aftershocks of her incredible orgasm still trembled through her. Ryder had sneaked past her boundaries, ridden beyond the finish line she'd established, and gone for the gold with his incredible focus on her needs while suppressing his own apparent desire.

She shouldn't let need sway her resolve to keep things professional once they exited the serene bubble of freedom the meadow had given them. "I don't know," she said, stroking his brow and dancing her fingers along his stubbled jawline. Though they'd get back to their reality in a day, she wanted to understand how he'd developed the incredible capacity to give so much.

And why he'd hidden it from the world with his

ridiculous string of shallow relationships when he could be the perfect man for someone.

Someone like her.

Not her, she reminded herself. Still, maybe they could be friends long after they went their separate ways. "But I liked it," she said. "A lot."

He laughed, then kissed her temples. "You'll like what I'm about to do a whole lot more."

His shaft jumped against her groin, and her sex ached with renewed need. "Really?" she asked, keeping her voice light. "You're ready to go the distance, but did you come prepared?"

He grinned, and the charmer in him lit up his beautiful eyes. "Like a boy scout."

Ryder shifted off her and she heard the rip of foil. He returned and she welcomed his powerful body back. A second later, his lips were on hers. And then he pushed into her in one long, deep stroke and filled her.

She lifted her hips to take him deeper, deeper still. Oh, he felt right inside her.

"Addison. You're so wet for me." He ran hot kisses over her mouth, her jaw, and on the sensitive skin at the base of her throat. "So fucking beautiful."

The exquisite ache between her legs intensified, and sent waves of pure ecstasy throughout her body as he moved in and out of her. Deeper, faster, and then slower, torturing the folds of her sex with the tip of his swollen cock head.

"Ryder. Don't stop." She might die if he didn't fill her.

"I don't just want to feel you come all over me," he said, plunging inside her and increasing his tempo. "I want you to come with me." His hands were all over her, cupping her breasts and teasing her elongated nipples into tighter points.

His sexy talk excited her. She felt possessed, owned, and branded by his sheer determination to claim her with his body. He pumped into her again and again. She contracted around his incredible, thick length. She'd never been with a man so rugged, raw, and commanding.

She loved it.

Loved being with him.

Loved him.

"Make me," she cried. "I want you to make

me..." *yours*. She was losing her mind, unable to think or fathom where she ended and he began.

She knew one thing. Him.

"Ryder," Addison cried, her orgasm building low and intensifying while he drove into her hard, fast, deep.

"Tell me you're with me."

"I am. Oh, I'm so there."

He plunged into her one last time, his eyes locked onto hers, with his release shuddering through him. Stars burst bright white and she crested over the edge with him. And when she fell back into herself, she struggled to shut down the longing she recognized in his gaze. One that matched her desire and the intense yearning for so much more.

To be cherished. And to cherish. To be adored. And to adore. To be loved. And to love.

To belong.

Chapter Eight

Addison stared at her desk top screen and reread the online tabloid's headline, then glanced at Ryder who had plunked down in her favorite comfy chair. "Please tell me this is the last of your ex-girlfriends with stories to tell," she said, then popped open her throat lozenge container and took one. After what she'd experienced almost a week ago with Ryder, she could certainly understand the trail of women who still wanted a piece of him. Most wanted to make bank on having been with him.

She, however, just wanted him. And the idea of all those perfect, skinny models being with Ryder resurrected her insecurities. Sure, she'd lost weight, and he'd been more than appreciative of the end results, but Addison was far from the perfection of the women he usually dated.

"I have no idea."

"Miranda Sinclair won't be easy to neutralize," she said. "And your other teammates can't share their up close and personal encounters with her, either. Half of them are on the 2016 Olympic squad."

"Coach Jamison won't go for it."

"Exactly. Ryder, we have to reconsider going to the media with the truth about what happened with Tiffany."

"No. I won't let Eric get dragged through hell again." Ryder sat straighter. "Use the team doctor's documentation. I always pass my drug and alcohol screenings."

"That'll help." But it wouldn't be enough. Not with the barrage of online tabloid accounts. They'd run with lies and innuendos to get ratings, but people fed on rumors like candy. "I'll get a news release out stating the facts, and up your appearances at local charity events." Then she'd contact Eric discreetly and determine for herself if he'd object to the full version of the story coming out. She owed Ryder to check first, but she owed her agency and her father her due diligence. She stood and stretched her arms high, wishing she could squash the ex girlfriend like a bug.

The logistics of protecting Ryder squeezed her thoughts until her head ached. How could she save him, and the agency's reputation, without losing Ryder's trust?

"You weren't drinking the night of the accident."

"Alcohol isn't my thing."

Dear Lord, she loved the way he filled out his corporate sponsor's jersey. Quickly, she averted her eyes and tried to focus on finding a fix to their current PR nightmare. Difficult when she had been with him, naked and together *all the way*. Even more, her heart had slipped, teetered on the edge when they'd made love last week. Because he was so good at using his body to please hers. At least, she kept telling herself that whenever she wanted another make out session with Ryder.

But she couldn't afford to let her heart buy into what her body kept telling her.

"Thanks," he said. "And thanks for believing me about the boozing bullshit before the reports came back from the doctor."

"That's why you're paying Carrington Agency our commission," she said, while inwardly warning her nipples to stay strong and not respond to the way his smoldering dark gaze held hers. "Besides, I've never seen you take one sip of alcohol. Not even when you were in university. Heck, even I got drunk a few times during college."

"I'm an athlete," he said casually. "My body is my temple."

"Oh baloney. If your body was your temple, you'd stay clear of monster cheeseburgers and french fries."

She grabbed the suit jacket she'd hung on the back of her chair and shrugged it on. Not only did she want to hide her arousal from Ryder, but she also wanted to understand why he made his choices.

"Maybe your background can help spin the press even more in your favor," she said, then crossed the room to stand in front of him. Her hormones did a happy dance. Bad move. She stepped back. "I might even be able to tie it into another charity event."

He'd been training non-stop since they'd returned from Saddle Creek, Montana, but Ryder had followed her PR directives. After she picked him up from the training course, he'd visited the numerous hospitals and community awareness events without complaint.

The man was a machine. Oh, what a machine indeed. *Stop. Stop. Stop. Stop thinking about the day in the meadow.*

Ryder lifted one end of his perfectly sculpted lips into a half smile. He knew damn well his effect on her. "Ryder," Addison said. "This is important."

He shrugged, then shot her a whatever kind of look. "Okay, here's the deal. My mom was a drunk," Ryder said. "She had no idea where I or my sister were from the time we were toddlers. I'm surprised Mom stayed sober during her pregnancies. If she did, that is."

"I see," Addison said. But really, she didn't. Nothing in her life experience compared to Ryder's shitty childhood. "What about your father? Why didn't he do something about it?" For all the problems she had with her own dad, she knew Alexander Carrington would never allow anyone to hurt her. He'd even shielded her from the pain of her mother's illness and death to the best of his abilities.

"My old man is why I spent two years at Saddle Creek Ranch," Ryder said, then tunneled his fingers through his hair.

The air bottled in her lungs while she absorbed Ryder's revelation. She waited several beats until she spoke. "You said you didn't have a juvenile record. Did he turn you in—like a tough love kind of thing?"

"Hardly. Love didn't play a role in what he did." He pushed out of the chair and moved to stand face-to-face with Addison. "He stayed in the cell next to me after our arrest."

He was so close she could see specks of indigo in his eyes, and more. The complete sense of I-dare-you-to-judge-me pulsed between them. "Were you guilty?" she asked.

"Of being in the wrong place at the wrong time. Yes. I drove his beat up Cadillac out of the parking lot after he held up a convenience store." Ryder didn't break eye contact. "My high school detentions didn't help my case, but my counselor testified on my behalf."

His voice was devoid of emotion. Oh, how she

hated hearing him this way. And, reading the lines bracketing his mouth along with the grooves marring his handsome forehead, she realized the memory was as fresh today as it had been fourteen years ago. Deep down, where it mattered, Ryder was still a kid who had been betrayed by the person supposed to protect him. No wonder he went beyond the call of duty to show the people in his life they could count on him.

"Why did your high school counselor go the extra mile for you?" She linked her hand with his, wanting to draw him out and yes, damn it, her heart yearned to comfort him.

A muscle jumped in his jaw. "He saw something in me. Plus, he knew I got into fights to make sure assholes stopped picking on my sister."

"You have spent your entire life looking out for everyone," Addison said, the dots in her brain connecting faster and faster. She'd make sure Ryder didn't pay the consequences for the accident that sent his career spiraling into the danger zone. "You ever wonder what it would be like to have someone look out for you?"

"I had someone." His grip tightened and he took

her other hand. "My high school counselor and John were friends—when John still worked as a cop in Los Angeles in our school district. Dude pulled some strings, and I got sent to Saddle Creek Ranch."

She squeezed his broad palms. "That's where you learned how to be a champion."

"That's where I learned how to be a man of honor." Ryder pulled her closer to his chest. "But I've made my mistakes."

"No one's perfect. Not even you," she said, then rested her head against his shoulder. Oh, how she loved the integrity which had driven Ryder to risk his career and his reputation for his friend and his family. But the tabloid storm wasn't going anywhere and she needed to quadruple her efforts to stop it now.

He released one of her hands and stroked her hair until he caressed her nape. "You deserved better from me. I should have protected you from those assholes."

"That's over. This is now. I know what kind of pressure you were under back then." She glanced at him through her lashes. "For what it's worth, what happened forced me to face myself and quit drowning my feelings with boat loads of chips, chocolate, and ice cream." Though the former fat girl in her still lived deep inside, Addison had come a long way from that person.

Just as Ryder had come a long way from the teenager that trouble had a habit of finding.

"Your willpower is pretty damn amazing," he said hoarsely.

Oh, with food, yeah. She could say no to a tub full of ice cream. Easy. But Ryder? His body sent all kinds of electrical charges through her and her body hummed with need. And her heart yearned to connect with his... in the one way to satisfy her craving.

"True," she said. "However, I've realized I can't get enough of one thing."

"What?" he asked.

"You." After all, who would discover she'd fallen off her do-not-touch-Ryder-wagon in the sanctity of her home? Nice, safe, and away from the limelight.

***

Ryder exhaled a breath, then angled Addison's head upward and brushed his lips over hers. "Me, either."

He held her gaze and read more than need in the fathomless depths. Amber and emerald prismed a rainbow of longing and desire in her beautiful hazel eyes. "I can't stop thinking about you. Whenever I'm in the same room with you, I remember how amazing you were when I was inside you. Living with you, sleeping down the hallway from you instead of sharing your bed, is driving me crazy."

Her lips parted ever so slightly. "Crazy is an understatement where I'm concerned."

"I don't break promises." However, in this case, he seriously reconsidered his I'll-do-anything-to-have-you vow on a continual basis all week.

"I'm the Queen of the PR spin." She traced her fingers down his jawline, and rained small kisses across his cheeks and mouth. "How about we place a moratorium on the promise while we're alone? Only stick to it while we're out in public?"

His cock hardened. And those tiny kisses made his blood run hot. Wanting her hadn't surprised him. The desire to connect at a deeper level, and his intoxicating need for her had caught him off guard. He couldn't even erase the intense craving during his training sessions.

A first.

"No PDAs works for me." He pressed his rock hard shaft against her. "But I want to touch all of you, make you come for me and with me, whenever we're alone."

"*Ryder.*"

Everything he wanted deep down resonated in her voice—an unspoken plea for so much more than sex. His need mirrored in her gaze.

"I can't get enough of you." Ryder twisted her long, beautiful and silky blonde hair in his hands, and turned her face up toward his. Her lips parted, and the pulse in the hollow of her throat fluttered wildly. "I don't know if I ever will."

He'd never had such a deep connection with a woman. And the world seemed to shift under his feet after he'd confessed the truth to Addison. He didn't want to hear her response—not if it wasn't what he thought he'd read in her eyes. So he locked his lips onto hers, and lost himself in the way her body answered him.

Addison skimmed her palms along his back and

circled his neck, clinging to him while he slicked his tongue with hers. She melded perfectly into his. Addison made him long for something he'd fought against wanting his entire life. She had cracked past his guard years ago with her sweet, giving nature. Then she'd shown him days ago her generous, loving heart still existed.

That heart held the promise of snuggling together while watching the ocean crash onto the shore. That heart held the key to allowing him to be at his most vulnerable and trusting her to accept him 100 percent. That heart held the secret to having a future filled with family, friends, a lifetime together.

He was terrified of breaking that heart again. But he couldn't stop himself from reaching for it one more time.

"Addison," he said, wrenching his mouth from hers. "I want to have you—all of you. Here. Now."

"That makes two of us."

The last of his self-control evaporated, and he kissed her with all he had inside him. More. He had to have more of her. He wanted to touch every last inch of her skin with his hands, his mouth, his entire body.

He skimmed the length of her back, unzipped her pencil skirt, and jerked it down her hips until it puddled around her shoes. She moved to toe them off. "Leave them on," he said hoarsely while tugging her cream-colored silk shirt over her head.

His breath caught in his throat when he took in her see-through bra and lacy thong. "You're beautiful." He cupped her breasts, felt the hard points of her nipples against his skin. "So responsive." And she'd been made so perfectly for him that his chest hurt.

He lowered his head to suck in a nipple through the fabric. Her gasps filled the air and she twined her fingers in his hair. "Oh. My. God."

"That's it, sweetheart." Ryder moved to her other breast and teased the rosy bud with his teeth, then slicked his tongue across her bra. "Let yourself go with me." And only him. For now, and forever. But he didn't articulate the thought. No way would he jinx this moment when he was so close to being right where he belonged all over again.

He lowered his head, sliding his tongue from her sensitive breasts lower, and lower still until he reached the apex of her thighs. Her sweet scent of honey and spice enveloped him. She smelled so damn good—he knew she'd taste even better when she came all over his mouth.

Kissing her sexy panties, he slid his finger under the thin strap of fabric between her sex's slick folds and pushed it into her wet heat.

She trembled and her hips hitched. "I don't... I mean I've never..."

"You've been missing out," he said, easing another finger into her and pushing it deep while edging her around until the backs of her legs nudged her oversized chair. "Let me love you with my tongue, Addison." With his tongue and his entire being.

She sank into the seat. "Only you."

"Yes." He lifted her long legs over his shoulders and kissed her sweet spot. "Only me." Knowing no other man had done this to Addison sent a surge of possession through him. He loved that he was her first lover *this way.*

Ryder shifted the pretty panty aside, and pressed his lips onto her throbbing bundle of nerves. Her clitoris jumped and her velvety warmth convulsed around his fingers. Soon. After he made her come, he'd slide his cock into her and give them both what they needed, wanted, craved.

He slicked his tongue over her sex, licking and tasting her essence while driving his fingers deep. She writhed on the chair, and the heels of her sexy shoes dug into his back. Christ. She tasted so good. Tangy, tart, yet oh, so fucking sweet.

Her hips bucked, but he pinned her with his free arm. "Don't fight it, sweetheart," Ryder said, taking his mouth away long enough to look at her flushed skin and the passion glazing her eyes. "Let yourself go. I've got you."

"Ryder. Please." She held him close to her sex. "I want you."

"I know." Ryder slid his tongue along the seam of her moist folds and across her clit. "I can't wait to drive my cock into you after you come for me. I want to feel how much you want me."

A shudder traveled through her body. "Ryder," she cried.

The first waves of her orgasm pulsated against

his tongue and flowed over his fingers. He held her and drank her in, savoring the intoxicating flavor of her release. And finally receiving what no other man had ever been given.

Her trust.

Chapter Nine

Addison scanned the mountain trail descending at an angle, which had her wondering how Ryder ever completed a race in one piece. This fifteen-mile mountain bike loop didn't even come close to matching the challenging courses he'd aced time and time again, but it didn't stop her from worrying. Her recent phone call to Eric Langston doubled her anxiety—but the tabloid monster verging to pounce loomed. She had no other choice.

To distract herself, she private messaged her camera crew to move closer to the finish line. Putting her energy on what she could control kept the edge off her concerns.

The first trio of racers appeared on the mountain ridge, and the crowd around her began whistling, and blowing horns. The announcer's voice called out the names of the top three cyclists. Ryder's lead at the top of the list.

Adrenaline rushed through her, making her fingertips zing and her heart pump wildly. "Make sure you get him as he crosses the finish line," she called to her crew while moving through the crowd of people laughing and ringing cowbells.

Excitement filled the air. Rock music played in tandem with the athletes who shimmied their bikes between tall pine trees and around manmade giant slalom markers. So fast. So dangerous. He cruised down, down, down until she couldn't even feel herself breathe. Ryder controlled his bike with the same finesse and skill he used as a lover.

Determined.

Strong.

Focused on the end result.

The sun rays reflected off Ryder's helmet as he approached the goal posts at a speed that defied explanation. She couldn't see his eyes behind the wraparound dark glasses covering them, but she didn't have to when she already had first hand knowledge of the intensity in his gaze.

Today he zeroed his attention on the win. Last night, he'd zeroed the same impressive attention on her.

"Go. Go. Go," she shouted with the rest of the fans as Ryder zoomed through the goal posts and finished first with a kick out jump that pushed the back all-terrain tire to the side.

Her photographers shot the film, and dozens of people raised their phones to capture the winning moments. Her heart stuttered in her chest as he unclipped his shoes from the bike and disembarked. He was, in a word, gorgeous. Ryder handled the fans pressing in around him with his easygoing, natural charm—pausing to kneel and give the younger fans his autograph, letting sexy young women with barely there shorts and skintight T-shirts scoot in next to him to take selfies, and high fives from his competitors. Suddenly, a chill traveled down her spine despite the warm California afternoon sunshine baking the south side of the mountain.

This was Ryder's world. One filled with babes called *Bettys* and powerful athletes who lived hard, played hard, and rode hard.

Addison tugged her conservatively cut shorts and glanced down at her preppy boat shoes. She didn't belong in this world. She didn't fit. She doubted she'd ever feel comfortable with the aura surrounding Ryder.

Eventually, he'd grow tired of being with her and move on to reclaim the life he had before the accident which forced him into hers. Her world meant making sure her father's top client stayed on top. With that in mind, she jerked her iPhone out of her cross-body leather satchel to text her father with the good news, and to offset his last message demanding answers about the ongoing negative press swirling around Ryder.

She'd pull out her last recourse if necessary.

But before she could punch in the message, he lifted her into the air and without preamble Ryder's mouth locked onto hers and gave her a full-on toe curling kiss that knocked the wind out of her lungs. Over and over, his tongue tangled with hers while he twirled her round.

Her muscles went slack and the phone slipped from her hand. Instinctively, she answered the demands of his lips. She tasted salt and mint and man. Oh, how she loved the feel of his arms holding her high, and the power of his possession. Everything in her called to him.

Dimly, she heard people yelling *Ryder's got a new Betty* and the electricity charging into her erogenous zones scattered. No. No. No. She wasn't anybody's *Betty.*

She wrenched her mouth from his. "Stop." Addison's pulse still beat fast for Ryder, but she couldn't let this kiss continue. "This isn't what I want in the tabloids or splashed all over the Internet." Especially not until she had a chance to figure out how to convince Eric to step out of the shadows and into the limelight for Ryder.

A muscle jumped in his handsome, stubbled jaw. "It was a victory kiss," Ryder lowered her to the ground. "Got caught up in the moment."

She stepped out of his embrace and scraped her fingers through her hair. They'd both gotten caught up in the rush of adrenaline that followed Ryder's win. "You promised no PDAs," she said quietly. "No telling what kind of fall out will happen because we couldn't control ourselves in public."

"You worry too much."

"It's my job to worry where you're concerned." She knelt and picked up her iPhone, then read the screen. Crap. Four texts. One from her contact in the LAPD confirming Ryder's story and a promise to follow up with the witness list. Three from her father. Two with information about another one of Ryder's ex-girlfriends going for her fifteen seconds of fame with tell-all exclusives about his past—stories which would reveal his record and the crapshats he had for parents.

The last one a virtual scream written in all-caps and a string of exclamation marks. Her father had put Ryder in her supervision because he'd been sure his daughter would never be the kind of woman his star client screwed around with ever.

Addison pursed her lips, then pointed at the reason for all four texts. She wanted him to be seen with the charity fundraiser's organizers, not her. The appearance would offset whatever his ex had to say. Bad boy gone good. Except with her. She sighed. "Go hang out with your fans, Ryder. I've got to troubleshoot this situation." And pull out the last big gun she had to put all the rumors and innuendos to rest.

"Whatever you say." Ryder tucked a strand of her hair behind her ear. "But I have a feeling you're not worried about saving my reputation. You're freaked out about me screwing up yours."

Her throat ached. Everything they had worked for hung in the balance. The only way to save Ryder's ass from the vultures circling around him had been to pursue the one thing he'd asked her not to do.

"You have no idea what I'm dealing with," Addison said.

"That's because you don't tell me anything."

He turned away and walked toward the podium where the announcer shouted out the race times. Casual, cool, controlled. Anyone who didn't know Ryder wouldn't see the frustration ripping in the muscles of his broad shoulders.

Those shoulders carried far too much. Now she'd lift the burden once and for all.

Yes. She'd promised not to reveal the truth about what had happened the night of the crash. But sometimes promises had to be broken for the better good. Protecting Ryder meant taking a risk that she'd destroy his trust, but she hoped her skills in negotiation and spinning stories wouldn't lead to that happening.

***

Within twenty-four hours, the picture of Ryder kissing Addison had gone viral. By the following Monday, the latest shit story perpetuated by Miranda Sinclair had leaked to anyone who would pay for the information. Addison had tentatively brought up the possibility of coming forth with the truth about the accident, but he'd waved it off. Asking her to prove she could do it without involving Eric. Then, after he'd shown up on the training course early Wednesday morning, Coach Jamison had arrived with an ultimatum. Win the pre-Olympic qualifier or lose his spot on the Rio de Janeiro cycling team.

There wasn't room for one more fuck up in his personal or professional life.

He landed his bike on the packed dirt of the training trail, then performed a reverse wheelie while rolling the front tire forward. Tricks. Landings.

Speed. All of the elements were practiced until his entire muscle system remembered to perform even when his brain failed to execute.

Ryder zoned out to his favorite band playing heavy metal through his earbuds while he took the next vertical drop. A gonzo of epic extremes. Treacherous to the best athletes in his league, but nowhere near as dangerous as trying to keep his heart on a short string whenever he hung around with Addison.

Which wasn't often. Sure, they managed to sneak in more rounds of awesome sex, but that wasn't enough anymore. He wanted all of Addison. He'd been more freaked out about it than he wanted to admit, but damn it. Why couldn't he have her?

He increased his speed, and the wind snapped like dozens of sails catching air. But he rode in the center of the storm, beating it and going faster, faster, faster until he crossed the end of the line.

"What's my time?" he asked his coach when he cruised to a stop.

"Clocked a record breaker," Jamison said. "Repeat this performance in July's Pro Gravity qualifier, and you'll nail your spot on the team."

Ryder took the towel Jamison held and swiped his face. "I plan on it."

"Good. Now that you've got a handle on your personal shit I can't see any roadblocks to keeping your sponsors in line."

"I hired the best." He'd satisfied his coach, but frustration gnawed at him. "She's the Queen of PR." Addison had busted her ass to spin every new publicity problem into something positive. Her hard work, and beating his original gold winning record, should have made him freaking happy. But instead he found himself questioning her motives.

Ryder wanted to believe Addison had gone the extra mile for him because she genuinely cared about him. But she had been closed lipped about her next PR push, and the constant texts from her father had her sucking more cough drops than he'd believed humanly possible.

Was she saving him, or was she saving herself?

*** 

"I'll take care of this," Addison said to her father on her home office's speaker phone. "Like I've lobbed all the other PR nightmares crawling out of the gutter to take a hit on Ryder."

"Miranda Sinclair isn't going away. And his parents are liabilities. Big time."

She sucked on her cough drop, then crunched down hard. "He can't control what his parents do. That's not his fault."

"Fault doesn't matter when a story is juicy and the media makes him look like he's abandoned dear old dad and mom."

Addison sighed, then opened the folder on her desk. She had witnesses, a police toxicology report, and a widower who wanted to do right by his friend and former teammate. But first, she had to give Eric time to explain things to his sons. "I've got this, Dad."

"You better have it, or Ryder will lose everything," he said in a firm, no-nonsense tone. "The mark of a great PR agent is one who puts the client's future above all else. Even if the client is too horse-assed to agree. Do I have to return to Los Angeles to hammer out a counter offensive?"

"No." She popped another cough drop. "I've got

a fix."

"Something to satisfy the sponsors?"

"Absolutely."

Addison ended their call, then closed the folder and tucked it under a stack of paperwork. Standing, she mentally ran through the scenario she'd orchestrated. Late afternoon sunlight filtered through her floor to ceiling windows and she walked toward them to look at the view below.

One with more than miles of ocean and beach sands sparkling with the reflections of seashells. One with the lone figure of a man walking along the shoreline. Ryder. The brilliant sunshine highlighted his tousled dark hair, and water slapped his bare feet while he strolled the beach's length.

Glorious, wonderful and quite possibly the best person she'd ever met.

But she'd kept him at bay emotionally ever since the damn public kiss. Even when they'd stolen moments together—sexy, fun, beyond amazing moments—she'd been afraid to expose her heart to him.

Not when the repercussions about what she had

pulled together loomed.

"I have to do it." She touched the glass separating her from the only man she'd ever loved. "For you."

Though it killed her to override Ryder's wishes, Eric had been all too willing to give an interview with the top talk show host in Los Angeles. Addison had given Eric the option to bury the details, but he'd known about Tiffany's alcohol and drug abuse along with her ongoing affairs with anyone who still reeked of fame. He'd also been close to serving divorce papers and filing for full custody before the wreck had claimed her life.

Addison had scheduled the interview for July fourth. Independence Day could either bring closure, or it could go up in smoke. But she had total confidence it would torpedo the negative press about Ryder, and she had a plan in place to shield the Langston children from any fall out. Now Addison prayed that once she explained Eric's motivation that Ryder would realize her decision remained the best way to proceed for everyone involved.

But first she had to show Ryder she cared.

CHRISTINE GLOVER

Chapter Ten

A pair of terns zigzagged ahead of Ryder while he walked alongside the waves ebbing and flowing onto the shoreline. Today's training session had been grueling, but once more he'd shown Coach Jamison he had the greatest potential to bring home the Olympic gold medal from Rio de Janeiro in August.

A month ago, winning the gold would have been enough.

Not anymore.

He heard Addison call his name and shifted his gaze toward the wooden staircase that connected her home on the high cliff to the beach. She stepped down the planks with a blanket folded over her arm and a straw tote bag in her hand until she reached the bottom.

The breeze coming in from the ocean lifted the

hem of her peach colored dress and gave him an awesome view of her long legs. His pulse went from zero to a sixty in an instant. Christ, she was beautiful, inside and out. She never gave up on a person, ever. Not even him despite the media shit storm swirling around him.

She closed the remaining distance between them, flared open the blanket and settled it on the beach. "Figured you could use a carb pick me up after training all day." Addison lowered herself to the covered ground. She dug into her tote bag and withdrew two water bottles and tossed him one. "I brought chips."

"Salt and Vinegar?"

"Your favorite brand."

"Trying to tempt me into doing another photo op?"

She slanted her gaze toward him. "We're finished with all the promotions until after your race." Addison leaned back on her elbows and lifted her head to let the sun dance on her skin. "Once you win, we're golden."

Her nipples poked through the fabric of her sheer

dress and he could make out the V of her bare sex. His cock hardened and blood rushed to the throbbing head. "Addison." He struggled to string together coherent words. He didn't just want sex, he wanted it all. With her.

A month ago making out with a woman like Addison with no strings attached would have been more than enough. He'd never seen himself as a permanent commitment kind of guy. Not with the shit example of marriage his parents had paraded.

But now he could imagine being with her in all the ways that mattered.

She shielded her face with her hand. "Yes?"

"I don't want potato chips."

"What do you want?"

The atmosphere between them thrummed with electricity. Tiny particles of sand and dust and shell floated in the air while his heart banged against his sternum. "You." He sat beside her and covered her hand with his. "I want every delectable inch of you."

Her pulse fluttered in her throat and her hazel eyes turned molten green. She'd bared herself to him body and soul only to guard her emotions after he'd blown her rule about no public PDAs. But now her heart shimmered in her expressive eyes.

"All of you, Addison." He controlled the desire to take her fast and hard and quick. Instead, he kissed her shoulder and slowly traced the curve of her lips with his index finger. "You think you can give that to me?"

"Yes."

The rush of blood thundering in his ears obliterated the crash of waves. There was only him. Only her. Only the promise of so much more than he'd ever expected mere weeks ago.

\*\*\*

Ryder's eyes gleamed hot on hers. "I want you with me. Always."

Addison's breath caught in her throat. *Always.* The overwhelming desire to show him how much she loved him tangled with practicality. Practicality won by a thin margin.

She had to tell him about her deal with the talk show, but before she could speak, he replaced his index finger with his mouth and traced her lips all over again with his tongue. And when he sucked in her lower lip, caressed the length of her body with his broad palm, her reason evaporated.

Ryder slipped his tongue inside her to deepen their connection. He tasted like sunshine, citrus, and all man.

She trembled, and wrapped her arms around his torso, drawing him closer. The scent of her arousal mingled with the ocean's, salt and tang carried by the ever-present breeze. He skimmed his hand under her dress's hem and brushed his fingertips between her legs until he slid them along the seam of her slick sex.

His erection throbbed against her hips, and the glide of his thumb over her clit sent electrical shocks through her. Every last inch of her wanted him on her, in her, taking what she wanted to give.

He lowered his mouth to rain soft kisses down her neck to the hollow of her throat, licked the wildly beating pulse while sliding her straps off her shoulders with his free hand to expose her breasts. "You're amazing." Ryder caressed the tight points with thumb and index finger one by one.

"You make me feel…" cherished, adored, beautiful.

He lowered his mouth to sweep his tongue across her nipples, kissing them and sucking while teasing her pulsating clit in tandem. Exquisite, delicious zings fired along her cells and she ached for the release only Ryder could give.

He kissed his way back up to her cheeks, her temples, and her brow. "Tell me." Ryder gazed at her with such intensity that she recognized how much his need mirrored hers. "You make me feel... loved."

"Because I do love you."

Heat pricked behind her eyes, and a sob filled her throat. Everything she'd guarded broke free. Her dreams, hopes, wishes for so much more than the life she'd carved out for herself slipped out of the mental cage she'd trapped them in. "Ryder." She feathered her fingers along his shadowed jaw and across his full lips. "I love you so much. I need you to understand that what I've done is because I love you with all my heart." Her vision blurred, and her tears tracked down her face.

She started to tell him about her plans, but he melded his mouth with hers. She tasted the salt of her tears, and the hot, hot need building between them with the glide of his tongue against hers. He caressed, teased, and explored her curves as if discovering her body for the first time.

She matched him touch-for-touch, pulse-to-beating-pulse, baring his body while he stripped her naked. Together, they sheathed his erection, silently and quickly.

He hovered over her, and nudged his cock between her slick folds. "I love how you feel when I'm inside you. So hot. So wet. For me."

"Only you, Ryder. I'm this way for you."

Addison brought her mouth to his, wrapped her legs around him and he plunged into her all the way to the hilt. He filled her, completed her in ways she'd never known. Pleasure melded with sweet pain as he drove into her over and over, bringing her close, and closer still to the release they both craved.

Skin slid against skin, hips raised and fell faster, faster, faster. He sent her higher, spiraling near the edge of her climax with his powerful, deep strokes. Addison called his name and clasped his shoulders, the sensations so intense she thought she might die.

But Ryder refused to let her go. "Come with me,

Addison. Show me how much you love me. Give me all you've got." He pushed deeper, stroked harder and she could feel the force of his orgasm throbbing in his thick length.

In her. For her. With her.

He drove into her, the power of his climax triggering a thousand star bursts behind her eyes. Her orgasm rocketed through her body, but this time, she crested over the final waves of incredible pleasure with Ryder. When she landed, she found herself right where she belonged.

In Ryder's arms.

Safe. Protected. Loved.

\*\*\*

Addison snuggled into Ryder and traced her hand down the length of his torso. A soft sigh of satisfaction escaped her lips as his muscles rippled beneath her touch. His arm tightened around her shoulders and she felt the press of his mouth on top of her head.

"You keep doing that and I won't make practice," he said.

"Mmm. True. Not to mention I have to save

some energy for work."

"I'm sorry about Miranda and the PR nightmare."

She painted tiny circles on the line of fine hair on his chest. Oh, how she wanted to draw out the pleasure that had carried them from their lovemaking on the beach all the way back to her home for more of the same in her bed.

All. Night. Long.

Her stomach dipped, and she stilled her hand. The passion they'd shared had been beyond incredible, but she had to face reality this morning.

Addison waited a beat, and swallowed hard. "There've been a few glitches, but nothing we can't handle." Like a coach who didn't want Ryder riled up and in danger of losing his focus, possibly injuring himself during practice runs, a father pressuring her to put the agency's reputation first, and a man who had asked for time to explain the unexplainable to his children.

He loosened his grip and propped up on his elbow to look at her. "What kind of glitches?"

"More lies about your past thanks to Miranda,

pictures of your mother dumpster diving, and your father's most recent mug shot surfaced." Addison stood and walked to her closet to grab her terry cloth robe. She slipped it on, and tightened the belt around her waist. "Carrington Agency has a counter offensive in the works."

Ryder shot out of bed, pulled on the board shorts he'd tossed to the floor the night before. "What kind of counter offensive?" He closed the distance between them to stand in front of her.

A razor's edge underscored his tone. She recognized his tell-tale stubborn set of his jaw all too well. A shiver ghosted down her spine and her skin prickled with goose bumps. Not good. So not good.

No more excuses. Ryder needed to know what she had planned. Still, now that they had admitted their feelings to each other, she had to believe he'd understand. Why wouldn't he? She'd done what she'd had to do to protect him and make sure he got what he deserved.

Love, and yes, damn it, responsibility toward her father's agency, had driven all her decisions and choices.

Holding his gaze, she took his hands in hers and prayed the love he held for her would drive his reaction. "The truth, Ryder. Eric's going public with what happened the night of the accident. This is our last chance to protect you."

He jerked his hands free, stepped back, and tunneled his fingers through his hair. "Fuck. You promised."

"Sometimes promises need to be broken for the greater good. I had to put your future first," Addison said, standing her ground. While she could respect Ryder for trying to cover up Tiffany's actions, she couldn't let him throw his career away for a lying, selfish woman who'd turned her back on her husband and family.

"The greater good had nothing to do with me." Ryder's eyes turned cold. "You were protecting Carrington Agency's top financial asset. And your own ass where your father is concerned."

"Money didn't drive my decision to approach Eric." No. The horrific tell-all news threatening to blast the Internet with more twisted half truths about Ryder had forced her to contact Eric. She'd shielded

Ryder from the possibility so he could focus on his future. One he'd earned and didn't deserve to lose.

"Bull. You want to prove to your father you'll do whatever it takes for Carrington Agency. I knew you were cold, but I sure as hell didn't think you'd railroad innocent kids and a grieving husband to guarantee your PR spin." He pounded his fist on his thigh. "Whatever you have planned, I expect you to squash it. Now."

Her pulse slowed to a sluggish dull thud in her ears, and spots flashed in her vision. She'd thought being called *Fattie Addie* behind her back had been humiliating, but it paled in comparison to Ryder accusing her of being a heartless bitch.

Where was the man who had held her when she'd been at her most vulnerable? Where was the man who had understood her deepest fears, and had shared a profound part of his own life? Where was the man who had confessed his love to her?

She pressed her palm onto her aching chest. Somehow she had to reach him. Otherwise, she'd have to do the hardest thing she'd ever done. "Yesterday, you asked me to give you everything," she said with a strength she didn't realize she possessed and despite the pain scraping down her throat. "I did. And because I did, I won't squash the one thing that will save your stubborn hide."

Ryder crossed his arms. "I'm an idiot for trusting you, but that ends today. Kill the campaign, or I'll sue Carrington Agency for breach of contract."

A vein pulsed in his temple and lines bracketing his lips brooked no argument. The threat stung, but no way would she let him see her flinch. "You'll lose." She channeled a little of her own inner steel and squared her shoulders. "I've done my due diligence, and the interview Eric's giving on Tuesday will prove Carrington Agency did exactly what you hired us to do."

"I thought you weren't an Ice Queen. That you were still the same, sweet person beneath your tough PR agent facade." Ryder shook his head. "No wonder you found a way to force Eric to do an interview that'll drag his family through the mud."

She should have told him about her carefully laid out plans before today, but Eric had asked her to keep the interview on Tuesday in the dark until he could explain what had happened to his children this weekend. Her desire to protect two little boys while giving Eric a way to find closure and move on to live the life he deserved had warred with wanting to tell Ryder the truth. Then when she'd tried to explain, he'd stopped her with his kisses and sweet seduction.

"Eric needed time to break the news to his sons."

"He wouldn't have needed to break anything at all if you'd kept your promise."

"You're jumping to conclusions about my actions, and I refuse to justify them to you." Her heart might shatter if he refused to listen. *Please let him realize she'd never do anything to hurt him.* "I fell in love with a man of honor. Someone who claimed he loved me. But if you really loved me, then you wouldn't doubt my motives. Without trust, we have nothing to keep us together but a business relationship."

"Business is all you care about."

His voice was devoid of emotion, and his face had transformed into an unreadable mask. Pain lanced deep and cut her to core for the man who refused to let anyone truly inside. "A long time ago, someone had enough faith in you to give you a second chance." Addison remained rooted to the hardwood floor. "Now you have to believe I have that same faith in you. Everything I've done is to show you that you're worth saving. But nothing I've done will matter if you don't ever learn to believe it yourself."

## Chapter Eleven

The climb up the fifteen-mile mountain trail's loop had been designed to deliver Ryder an unsparing body blow. He didn't give a shit. Sweat drenched his back, making his shirt cling to him and his feet had been waterlogged by the endless stream crossings. He still didn't give a shit. He only cared about blocking out the frustration, anger, and pain of Addison's betrayal.

But, as he cranked to the end of his ride, the Sierra Nevada wind lashing his skin without mercy, he tasted bitter defeat. Nothing had worked. Not getting out of Los Angeles with his assistant coach. Not escaping to his mountain retreat in the Sierra Nevada mountains. Not driving himself to train day in and day out—pushing the envelope harder than he'd ever pushed.

He failed miserably at obliterating Addison from his brain. And the hole in his chest had gotten bigger since he'd left her home in Los Angeles three days ago.

However, he had succeeded in shutting down all contact with the outside world other than checking his text messages. His home came into view, and Ryder cruised his bike toward the two-story log cabin that overlooked the pristine lake. The Sierra Nevada's snowcapped mountains reflected in the clear water, but the crisp air and stellar vista didn't lift his crap mood.

Ever since he'd packed his stuff and taken off for the mountains, his life had taken on a gray shade.

He missed her. Damn it all to hell. He missed the woman he thought he'd fallen in love with, not the Ice Queen who cared about the fucking bottom line.

A shower, brainless gaming on his computer, and mentally rehearsing for his next qualifier for the Olympics would take his mind off her. Thank God his assistant coach had given Ryder space, choosing to hole up in the guest suite above the four car garage.

That suited Ryder as he had no desire for human

contact.

He stowed his gear in the garage, then toweled off the worst of the grime while trekking to his kitchen. Grabbing a water bottle from his fridge, he heard his cell phone buzz on the granite counter behind him and turned to check his message.

Eric. He'd texted his friend to apologize for the hell Addison had asked him to face before the interview aired this morning.

*You catch the show?*

*Hell no.* The last thing he wanted to see was his friend get grilled by the most aggressive talk show host in Los Angeles. *Promise I'll make it up to you.*

*Nothing to make up. It's cool. Check out the recap on YouTube. Your girlfriend is amazing.*

*She's not my girlfriend.*

The annoying wait-for-text bubbles appeared, then disappeared, then reappeared. Finally, Eric responded. *Then you're a bigger idiot than I thought.*

What the fuck? *You don't have to defend her.*

*Watch the damn interview. TTYL*

He chugged his water, then crunched the bottle and tossed it into his recycling bin. He didn't want to see the fucking interview, but Eric didn't seem pissed about it, which surprised the crap out of Ryder.

Addison had asked him to trust her motives. But how could she possibly spin this right for Eric and his family? Only one way to find out. He ignored the dirt still remaining on his skin and pulled YouTube up on his phone.

Thirty minutes later, Ryder swallowed hard. Addison had orchestrated a PR miracle. For Eric. For his kids. And for Ryder. Idiot didn't even begin to describe Ryder. He'd fucked up royally in the worst way. Even worse, he'd accused the woman he loved of having the heart of a barracuda when in reality she had one of the most compassionate hearts he'd ever known.

Another text flashed. Rayne. He read the message and his throat closed around the lump that had formed during the last half an hour. The man who had taught him how to be a man, who had given him a way to succeed beyond Ryder's wildest dreams, had approached the end of his formidable life.

He'd given Ryder a second chance because he'd had faith in him.

Addison had said the same thing. She'd wanted him to realize he was worthy of saving. And because she believed in him, and loved him, Addison had simply asked him to believe it of himself. But that meant trusting her 100 percent and he'd never been the trusting kind. He'd rather fix his mistakes himself than admit he needed anyone.

Water, sweat, and fucking tears burned behind his eyes. He swiped them away and cursed himself for being the worst kind of fool ever.

He'd asked her to give him everything. She had.

All she'd wanted was for him to do the same.

Christ. He'd pushed away the only woman he loved. Stubborn, willful pride had blinded him to the gift she'd offered. He'd screwed up, but maybe, just maybe, he could convince her he was worth redeeming.

He had to prove she deserved a man who could make her forget her broken heart. Even if the man responsible was him. And if she could forgive him one more time, he'd spend the rest of his life showing her he'd been worth one last chance.

\*\*\*

Standing beside her father, Addison raised her binoculars to her eyes and searched the last stretch of the racetrack for Ryder. Six cyclists riding tire-to-tire vied for the top spot, shimmying around each other and between the pine trees. She spotted Ryder swerving dangerously close to the edge as he made a move to attack for the lead position. The force of his concentration and commitment to his sport, to winning, would never cease to stagger her. Her heart caught in her throat. He was, in a word, beautiful. The most amazing, generous hearted man she'd ever known. He put the needs of others before his own and now he was poised to reclaim Olympic gold.

Cowbells rang, and sirens wailed while people all around her screamed his name as he surged ahead of the other athletes. "Get closer to the finish line," she said to her live action crew. "I want footage of Ryder crossing."

"We'll want the usual. Victory walk, fans crawling for selfies, and accepting his trophy," her father added.

"I've got this, Dad."

"Sorry." He wrapped his arm around her

shoulders. "Old habits die hard."

She smiled. Her father had finally retired and given her full control of their family's company, but letting go of the reins would be an interesting transition. "I'm glad you're here," Addison said, meaning it. She'd been semi dreading coming to the qualifying race. Not sure if she could handle seeing Ryder after all that had happened between them.

But her father had called and asked to join her for their company's major victory lap with their star client. "I figured you could use a friendly face," he said. "Be proud of what you've accomplished, Addison. Your PR coup did more than salvage Ryder's reputation. Elite athletes are lining up for Carrington Agency to represent them."

Her final assault on the negative press attacking Ryder had exonerated him and solidified his positive, good guy image. Eric's interview about Ryder's desire to protect the Langston family had shown the public their athletic idol had a heart so big, so honorable, no one would ever question his integrity again. "I am. But then I learned from the best in the business."

She had accomplished she had dreamed of attaining. Her father's respect and admiration, and the helm of her agency, but she'd lost the one thing that mattered most. Ryder.

Still, she'd have done it all over again even though her heart ached. No matter what, she couldn't go back to the person she'd been before Ryder had become her number one client.

The whistling, cheers and yells accelerated and then the rush of man and machine sailed through the goal posts.

"Follow him." She broke free from her father, and ran after the bike with her crew. "Close ups. Action shots. Get it all. We want to build on the momentum we've created."

She chased Ryder with her PR team, pushing through the throng of fans. Ryder swerved his bike hard to the left, came to his signature stop and raised his fist in the air. And smiled his trademark grin. One with a guaranteed-to-please sticker on it, which had garnered millions of dollars in sponsorships.

He dismounted his bike, gave it to one of his coaches, and started walking through the crowd. She expected him to sign autographs for his younger fans and snap pictures with the dozens of *Bettys* following him from race to race. Instead, he continued without breaking stride.

"What's he doing? He can't do this." Her heart thudded. Why would he blow this opportunity now that he had exactly what he wanted, too?

She shot her dad a confused look. He shrugged and seemed completely unfazed by the current Ryder turn of events.

The crew moved into a semi-circle around her as Ryder approached. He removed his helmet and took the wraparound sunglasses off his dirt streaked, handsome face. The crowd seemed to take a collective sigh, and the cowbells stopped clanging when he finally reached her.

His eyes—as blue as the brilliant summer sky overhead and filled with so much yearning that her heart ached—locked onto hers. "You aren't following the script," she said, wanting to reach for him, but stilling her desire with a stern reminder he'd hurt her one time too many during her lifetime.

"Sometimes we have to go off script for the

greater good." Ryder tilted his head toward the camera person to her right. "You rolling this live? I don't want the world to miss one minute."

She nodded. "Absolutely. Per your instructions."

"Instructions?" Addison's knees wobbled. "Who gave you permission to hijack my staff?"

"Your father. It was part of my negotiations for the contract."

"Why?"

"Because I wanted everyone to see me go for a better prize than a trophy or a gold medal." He brushed a tendril of her hair from her face, and tucked it behind her ear. "Addison, I shouldn't have questioned you. I screwed up royally when I didn't trust you to have my back."

The genuine remorse in his voice sent a wave of warmth throughout her body. "Yes, you did, but you've got a reputation for being bull-headed."

A muscle twitched in his jaw. "I'll need a lot of help beating that rap," he said.

"You've hired the best agency in the country to help you."

"True." Ryder closed the scant distance between

them and slid his broad hands down her arms until he linked them with hers. "But I'm not sure I can keep on racing if I don't win the most important thing in the world to me."

"You'll ace the Olympics."

"I'm not talking about gold medals and trophies." He swallowed hard and tightened his hold. "You're my finish line. Without you, nothing else matters. You're the one I want to wake up next to in the morning. You're the one I want to share my life with now and tomorrow and forever. You're my last chance, my only chance."

Tears pricked behind her eyes and her nose itched. He'd taken a big risk by putting himself out there publicly—all of his hopes and wishes for them. Without any guarantee she'd yield. "I want to believe you, but…"

Fear flashed for a second in his gaze. "Please, Addison. Forgive me one more time." He dropped to his knees, then unzipped one of his jersey pockets, and withdrew a ring. "You have to believe me. You gave me everything when you gave me your heart. I screwed up, but I promise I'll spend the rest of my life showing you how much I love you."

Her pulse accelerated into hyper drive, and the tears she had banked rolled down her cheeks. He'd proposed in front of a live audience, his fans, and all his adoring *Bettys*. No one had ever gone to such great lengths for her. And she knew no one else ever would. "Ryder," she said. "I love you. I've always loved you."

"Is that a yes?"

Someone laughed, and a few people started clapping. Around her, the crew grinned, and when her gaze landed on her father's, his paternal love shined in his eyes.

"Yes."

He slipped the sparkling diamond onto her trembling ring finger, then stood and pulled her into his arms. "I love you," Ryder said, then he lowered his mouth onto hers and brought her back to the place where her heart had always belonged.

# *EXCERPT from The Marriage Ultimatum. Available now!*

Holding a cold compress to his leg, Stefano Durante limped through the doors of Mountain Brook, Georgia's local clinic. "Damn, that was a close call," he said to his cousin, Gian. A little too close considering the tree's branches could have speared him through the chest instead of his left thigh.

Gian shook his head. "You're lucky this happened in a tourist town and not at home in Italy. Otherwise our grandfather might have called you back and made you walk down the aisle pronto."

His taciturn grandfather's warnings to settle down before Stefano's adrenaline junkie ways killed him rang through his head. "Ever since the doctor's tests to determine why Nonno has been rapidly losing weight, grandfather insists that I 'get married, make *bambinos.*'"

"He's worried."

"We're all worried," Stefano said. And that meant he had to get with grandfather's program, or lose his position at the helm of Durante Enterprises. "But the idea of marriage—even to set grandfather's mind at ease—gives me virtual hives."

Gian nodded. "Doesn't help that every woman you've dated only wants you for your wealth, not because they actually care."

The last one had been just like his mother. *Dio.* "Why does Nonno insist on old-fashioned tradition when the only thing that matters is my business track record?" Though he couldn't blame the old man after what his father did just before he'd died in a fiery car crash.

Embezzling from the family coffers wasn't easily forgiven. Not even when Stefano had done everything in his power to prove to his grandfather that he'd never steal from Durante Enterprises. He had a lot to make up for because of his father's mistake.

"Your record could go up in smoke if this accident reaches his ears—he's a hard man to please."

"No kidding."

Pain shot through Stefano's leg and his head throbbed. The clinic's florescent lights buzzing seemed to get louder, increasing the agony pinging in his temples while he hobbled toward the admitting desk. "There's got to be another option other than a marriage of convenience. No way in hell I'm following in my father's footsteps," Stefano said. After all, he had suffered the consequences of his father's poor judgment from the time he had been two years old.

"Our grandfather might be dying," Gian said. "But perhaps the last deal you brokered in Las Vegas will prove you're responsible."

"Doubtful. It won't be enough to save our company if I don't make things work out with Phillip Anderson."

Behind the scenes, Stefano had labored tirelessly to ensure that Durante Enterprises continued to stay in the black. But his family's steel manufacturing company—with factories in Northern Italy, parts of Europe, and Canada—was in trouble and the only way to guarantee his family's future profits was to bring it into a new age of innovation. He'd secretly been negotiating a merger with the Information Technology entrepreneur without his grandfather's consent in the hope that he could convince the old man to let go of the family reins.

After another huge *no* from Durante's patriarch, Stefano had channeled his frustration into hang gliding near Anderson's corporate retreat in Northern Georgia. Then he'd address the situation in person with Nonno when he returned to Italy.

Unfortunately, he'd lost control of the glider and crashed.

Now Stefano surveyed the tableau of misery filling every corner of the anemic room. Battered chairs, old toys, and a small television that looked like it had stepped out of the last decade accentuated the poverty that was hiding behind the upscale resort Stefano had stayed in during the week.

Babies wailed, squirming in their mother's arms. Other children cried. Adults drooped in chairs, some clearly injured. Old men moaned and groaned in wheelchairs, and mothers cajoled toddlers with promises of feeling better. Stefano inhaled the odor of antiseptic, the sickness permeating the air, the faint stench of sweat and cleanliness melding together.

He pulled out his wallet, and drew out several

bills. "Give this to the front desk nurse as a donation, then find out who I need to contact about getting some decent furniture and televisions in this place." Every inch of him hurt, but Stefano welcomed the pain. It meant he had lived to see another day, unlike his father. Even now Stefano wondered what had led to the accident: his mother's multiple affairs or being fired from Durante Enterprises when his corporate theft had been discovered. Most likely both had played a part, but the crash had been ruled an accident.

"Sure thing."

Stefano leaned against the counter while Gian slipped the pretty brunette manning the desk the money along with a dash of his own special brand of Italian flattery.

Gian returned with a clipboard and a pen. "I've got the administrative director's information." He passed the board to Stefano. "Fill this out. I convinced the nurse to let you cut to the front of the line."

"That wasn't necessary. And completely unfair to the people waiting ahead of me," Stefano said, though nausea rose in his throat and the room spun.

Gian caught Stefano before he hit the ground. "It's a done deal. And you had better hope this godforsaken place is so far off the grid that grandfather's radar will miss it," he said.

"The man has eyes everywhere," Stefano said, scribbling information onto the forms while propping on the front desk for support.

Gian pulled his smartphone from his back pocket. "I'll check the Internet for any leaks about the accident just in case we need to do damage control."

Black spots danced in front of his eyes. "Good idea. This accident could screw up everything with Nonno." Not to mention, raise more flags about the company's financial vulnerability. If Anderson caught wind of this, he might take his money and his ground breaking software platform to one of Stefano's competitors. Didn't help that corporate piranhas had started circling around Durante Enterprises when rumors of his grandfather's declining health surfaced.

Stefano had to find a way to convince Nonno to give him full power over Durante Enterprises.

His back pocket vibrated as Gian looked up from his phone. "Sorry, cousin. Your luck has officially run out." He showed him the screen. "The crash went viral on the Internet."

"Shit." Stefano pulled out his phone and read the text from his grandfather's secretary. "Grandfather expects me to return to Italy after I'm treated for my injuries." He doubted the formidable man who had raised him would back down from his demands. "He'll cut me out of the business if I don't settle down immediately."

"Who does he have in mind?" Gian asked.

"No one yet, but I'm sure he'll find someone in his little black book of friends with eligible daughters." Today's hang gliding accident, and the resulting leg wound, had popped the last balloon in his permanently single and loving it ride.

Gian cringed while he quickly finished filling out the paperwork. "You might want to start looking for your own wife."

Stefano handed the clipboard back to the admission's nurse. "That'll have to wait until after I'm treated."

Stefano caught a flash of caramel-colored, wavy hair out of the corner of his eye, and scrutinized the woman sitting in the corner of the room, holding her little boy.

The tilt of her head, the soft curve of her cheek as she pressed it against her son's curls, held his attention. Something in the way she soothed the child sitting on her lap, caressing his back and weaving her fingers through his dark, curly hair stirred him. Before he acted on his curiosity, an attendant ushered him into a small room where the ER doctor and nurse examined his scrapes, cuts, and bruises.

"You'll need stitches," the doctor said, examining the gash on his thigh. "And I recommend a tetanus shot as a precaution."

"Do what you have to do," Stefano said.

"I demand to get in to see the doctor immediately." He heard a woman's sharp, high voice. "Matthew is in a lot of pain. He can't wait anymore."

Guilt thrummed through Stefano. He'd allowed Gian to use his affluence to get in and out of the clinic quickly. And he'd done so at the expense of a child who didn't have the same privileges.

"Gian, go tell the front desk nurse to bring the woman and child back here immediately. They can share my room."

"Sir, there are privacy laws," his nurse objected.

"Pull the curtain and it won't be an issue." He grimaced as the nurse plunged the needle containing topical numbing liquid into his leg. "I don't want the boy to suffer needlessly." And the mother fighting for her baby deserved a break.

"Gotcha," Gian replied.

Moments later, the attendant returned with the woman and child. "Momma, Momma," the little boy cried.

Stefano cringed as the nurse continued stitching his leg and glanced at the mother who held her screaming child. Red clay smudged the back of the little boy's dinosaur themed T-shirt and grass stains marred the child's red shorts. "Shh, Matthew. The doctor has to check your bump and make sure you're okay first."

Her voice had a familiar ring to it, reminding him of another woman's southern drawl whenever he brought her to the brink of reason and beyond. He raked his gaze over her, took in her luxurious long hair, which obscured her face while she kissed her little boy's head. Though she'd dressed in an ugly brown polyester uniform, the drab outfit failed to obscure her curvaceous body.

Stefano did a double take. He remembered that hair. Hair he'd once twined his fingers through. Hair that had spilled on the pillow and sheets beneath him, fanning across the silk.

He recognized the long tapered fingers stroking the little boy's trembling back. He remembered her touch. Even now a flash of their final night together blinded him to the rest of the people in the room. Stefano only had eyes for her.

It had been three years since he'd touched her. Sure, he'd had dozens of women since their crazy whirlwind two-week affair in Atlantic City, but he hadn't erased her memory completely. He'd wanted to—badly. Because she'd almost made a fool of him. "Roxy?" he asked, quickly noting the lack of a wedding band.

Her head snapped up and her silver eyes widened. Shock flashed in her answering gaze.

"Stefano." She raised her chin after several beats of silence. "I never expected to see you again after you dumped me three years ago without even leaving a sayonara note on my pillow."

"I had my reasons," he said while he waved the nurse away.

She tightened her hold on her son, her face flushed bright red and she pointed one Converse shoe toward the door she'd walked through. "Reasons you failed to share with me at the time."

"Just as you failed to share the truth about your past with me." He'd almost broken his first cardinal rule about women—never confuse sex with love— and nearly proposed.

Her lips narrowed into a razor-sharp line and her nostrils flared. "I might have left out a few details about my background, but that's because my family hasn't played a starring role in my life since I was sixteen years old," she said.

"What about your brother?" Stefano asked.

Roxy paled. "How did you find out about Doug?" she asked while Gian circled the small room and moved toward the door behind her.

"Standard protocol to run a background check on any woman who might become the mother of my children." Though he'd wanted to punt it, Gian had insisted that he not let her off the hook if only to satisfy any doubts Nonno would have about Stefano's fiancée.

"Doug isn't a part of my life." Roxy lifted her son higher. "But that doesn't matter now. If you'd really cared about me, you'd have given me a chance to explain. Maybe things might have been different for all of us."

Stefano tasted a bitter tang of acid. He had a lot of experience with women *explaining* their lies. Lies that were always accompanied by crocodile tears and emotional pleas for financial handouts. "You had two weeks to tell me the truth, but you deliberately withheld important information."

"I suppose I didn't measure up to your family's standards when you found out about mine, especially when my brother had a rap sheet, but I never did anything wrong and I sure as heck paid the price."

Stefano refused to back down. "It's not like I left you destitute. I showered you with expensive jewelry, which I'm sure you pawned along with the limited-edition Breitling watch you stole from me. I imagine you had plenty of financial capital to open your art studio in New York," he said. Which made her presence in a Podunk, United States of America emergency room completely surreal.

Roxy lifted a single brow and shot him a look of utter contempt. "You have no idea who I am, or a damn thing about my circumstances."

"Enlighten me."

"I already tried to three years ago when I found out..." She shook her head. "But you're right. I sold everything—to get my brother into rehab and pay off his dealer and..."

"And what?"

Fear flashed in her eyes. "It doesn't matter anymore." Roxy took a step back toward the room's door, her son still crying in her arms while the nurse bustled back to Stefano's gurney. "We'll wait outside."

Behind her, Gian glanced at the boy in her arms, raised his brows, and mouthed "what the hell?"

*What the hell* didn't begin to express the electricity crackling between him and the woman he'd been in a passionate love affair with three years ago.

"Don't be ridiculous," he said. Regardless of what he thought about Roxy, Stefano couldn't let her little boy suffer. "Your son needs help." He touched the nurse's shoulder, stopping her from stitching his gash. "Get the doctor and have him look at the boy, please."

"But your stitches," the nurse protested.

"This cut's not going anywhere. You can finish sewing me up later."

"Okay." The nurse shot Roxy a look. "This man's injury is far more serious than a bump on the head, but I'd rather see a parent err on the side of protectiveness than neglect."

"Thanks, Sheila."

The nurse left and Stefano focused his attention on Roxy, pointing to her sobbing son. "You're on a first name basis with the ER nurse," he said. "You a regular visitor?" A sudden rush of memories about his multiple stitches, bruises, and scrapes surfaced.

"He's had more than his fair share of high fevers as a baby," she said. "Now he's a rambunctious toddler who finds trouble faster than most kids his age."

Her comment reminded Stefano of his

grandparents' ongoing concerns for him. "What happened to him this time?"

"He fell off a swing set." Roxy kept her son's head pressed to her shoulder, sheltering the toddler from Stefano's scrutiny. "Sheila's right. You need attention now." She took another step, turning toward the door.

In that moment, he caught a glance of her little boy's tear-streaked face and all his mental gears clicked into place. Quickly, Stefano calculated the days and months since he had last been with Roxy. The toddler in her arms, his hair dark as his own, squirmed and pushed to escape.

Stefano could feel his pulse pumping in his wound. Instantly, he bolted off his gurney, disregarding the pain shooting through his leg, and rushed to grab Roxy's shoulder. "Stop," he said, his heart racing, his soul knowing what shouldn't be possible.

The little boy wiggled out of her grip, slipped to the ground, and charged straight into Stefano's legs. "Go away," he screamed.

Stefano swooped the hysterical toddler into his

arms. *Cristo* he was strong, twisting and crying and flailing his arms, punching and struggling for release. "Slow down, easy now," he said, wondering if this was how his grandfather felt every time Stefano had done much the same when he'd been a child.

He held the flailing boy at arms' length and gazed into his eyes.

Eyes that stopped him cold.

Eyes that he'd always recognize.

Eyes that mirrored his own.

"Give Matthew to me," Roxy demanded, moving toward Stefano.

His mind racing with a thousand thoughts, he brought Matthew's struggling body into his chest to hold him close and examine the child's features that so matched his own. A myriad of emotions played through his mind. Doubt, astonishment, frustration. Tenderness. "Not before you explain," he said though he couldn't possibly be this boy's father. Hell, he'd successfully dodged half a dozen paternity suits because he always used precautions. But there was no denying his uncanny resemblance to Matthew or the timeline Stefano had mentally drawn from the last night he'd slept with Roxy.

"Momma," Matthew cried, twisting to escape Stefano's arms.

She raised her chin, disdain colored her eyes gunmetal gray as her gaze traveled from the top of his bruised forehead all the way down to the torn fabric of his once pristine white T-shirt. She continued looking all the way down to the legs where his designer jeans had been slashed open to access the wound still requiring stitches, and then back again to lock with his eyes.

"You said it yourself, Stefano. The time for explanations ran out three years ago. Though I sure as hell tried to contact you only to have your cousin block all my calls and emails." She shot Gian a look of pure hatred. "You're why Stefano didn't know about Matthew. But I doubt he'd have believed me, either, given that dang background check you ran."

"Gian?" Stefano asked. "You knew about this child?"

"I knew a liar called and said she was pregnant. I chalked it up to another lie. Or she'd gotten knocked up with another man's baby." His cousin didn't flinch at Stefano's harsh tone. "I spared you the trouble of dealing with it."

Roxy's gray eyes traveled between Stefano and Gian. Confusion and a hint of fear clouded her gaze while lines furrowed her brow. "I'll spare you the trouble of dealing with it today." She reached for Matthew and he tumbled into her arms. "Get your stitches and leave Mountain Brook, Stefano. The time for you to be here for us has long passed."

With that last parting shot, she turned on her brown Converse sneakered heel and walked out of the door and away from him, while maybe carrying the one thing that might save Stefano's daredevil ass from his grandfather's ultimatum. A moot point if Phillip Anderson took his ingenious ideas and technology somewhere else. There'd be no way to save Durante Enterprises from a massive corporate takeover if that happened. And the threat had become ominous once rumors about his Nonno's inability to continue as the CEO began swirling.

Even more, now that he'd discovered he might have a son, Stefano had a bigger reason to make the merger work. If Roxy wasn't lying, she'd handed him a solution to placate his grandfather and guarantee Durante Enterprises' future.

* * *

Roxy's heart pounded in her ears. In sixty seconds flat her road through life almost transformed from a Highway to Heaven to a Drive to Disaster. Clutching Matthew to her chest, she willed her racing pulse to slow. Then she checked the bump on Matthew's head one more time. "He'll be fine," she told the nurse at the front desk, eager to escape the clinic and Stefano Durante. For now. "Big mistake coming here." Especially since she'd already missed one too many shifts at Burt's BBQ and Sandwich Subs. Minimum wage wasn't great, but the tips were usually good and supplemented her daily living expenses along with boosting her cache of art supplies.

"Wait," Stefano called, chasing after her. "We need to talk."

She'd made many mistakes during her twenty-six years, and had paid a huge price for a few of them. But Roxy had given up on bridging the gap between her and Stefano when she couldn't break through his communication wall. Now he wanted to talk? Here?

"I can't." Still, the look of awe that had flashed in Stefano's brilliant blue eyes when he recognized Matthew's matching gaze stirred something deep inside her. Something she'd buried and had never dared to feel again.

Until today.

Unexpectedly meeting the father of her child here in Mountain Brook in the good old U S of A did more than freak her out. It resurrected old wishes and dreams that had gone tumbling down the proverbial cliff the minute she'd realized that she'd never be good enough for a man like Stefano. Not when she had a drug addict-slash-con artist for a brother, and the pedigree of roadkill possum.

It also resurrected old fears. Fears that might expose her to her brother's twisted schemes again. She didn't dare let Doug discover that she'd had a child, especially one that had a billionaire for a father.

She turned to face Stefano. "You need to finish getting stitched up first. Plus, I can't afford to dawdle around and chat," Roxy said calmly though her blood roared in her ears. "I've got to get to my job for the night shift." She also needed time to think and plan and figure out what to do.

"But the boy—you can't go away now that I know he might be mine."

Heat flashed through her body. That Stefano questioned the truth that had stared him in the eyes-only moments ago angered her, and cut her to the core. "Still have your doubts about me? Well, too bad," she said. "You're no longer relevant to my life."

"That's unacceptable."

"Deal with it," she said. "My life might not matter to you, but I won't risk everything I've done to rebuild it after you derailed it." Granted, she had no doubt that Stefano was Matthew's biological father, but that's where the Daddy train stopped. She refused to let Stefano get involved in her life when the repercussions could be dangerous.

"I thought you'd have one after you sold the jewelry I gave you... pawned my watch." Stefano inched closer to her. "What happened to all the money?"

"Ask your wingman, Gian," she said, suddenly tired with the weight of more than just her son.

Nearly every dime had gone to pay off her brother's dealer. Doug, unrepentant, had vamoosed into thin air shortly afterward, and some very scary men had tracked her down afterward to demand even more money. Knowing they meant business, she'd scraped together the cash by pawning Stefano's watch. She'd thought they acted alone, but she quickly discovered that Doug was in charge, and had scammed her with his threats. Six weeks later she'd discovered her pregnancy. That's when she'd decided to take off and start over in the small tourist town.

"We have to talk," he said again.

"There's nothing to discuss."

Roxy opened the clinic's main door with her hip and stepped into the afternoon sunshine. No way was she dealing with Stefano now, or ever. And she had to get to work, or she might lose her job.

She heard him order Gian to stay inside the hospital, and the sound of his steps following her out. Dang it, the man was persistent. Of course, that was how he'd suckered her into bed in the first place.

Roxy walked briskly to her small, compact ten-year-old blue car, and pretended not to hear him call for her to stop. Though a part of her did want to listen—the part that had been irrationally drawn to Stefano the night she'd entered the casino and looked for her older brother to convince him to get rehab. Man, had she learned a hard lesson as a result. One she'd use today to hold her ground.

"I'm as surprised as you are by this sudden meeting," he said, catching up with her and matching her stride for stride, his slashed jeans flapping in the wind which exposed his long, muscular legs. "But you will hear me out."

She inhaled his clean, masculine scent and could feel the heat emanating from his muscular body. Even now her long dormant hormones raised a hallelujah chorus at the mere sight of him. *Down girl. This is not about you, it's about Matthew's future.* "I won't," she said.

Her cell phone vibrated in her pants back pocket. Roxy shifted Matthew to her other hip, hauled out the phone and read the text. Her boss Burt demanding to know when she planned on getting her skinny behind to work.

Quickly, she responded with one hand, then

looked at Stefano's profile. Regret etched lines in his handsome brow, and he scrubbed a hand over his face. What she would have given to have him make things better way back when she'd been desperate for him to reply to her frenzied emails and texts. But then he'd never received them. Oh, she'd like to punch Gian in the nose for blocking her attempts to reach Stefano.

"I'm not going anywhere," he said.

Heat flashed through her body. Now she'd like to punch Stefano and throw in a kick for good measure. He had no right to interfere in her life, especially when she had no desire to jeopardize Matthew's safety. "No. But I am." Roxy squared her shoulders and continued to march along the sidewalk. *Pretend this nightmare hasn't happened. Keep moving until he goes away. Far, far away where he can't do anything to hurt us.*

"I won't let you near my son," she said, then looked into Matthew's eyes, the blue-green color matching Stefano's, his chubby toddler boy face sporting the same full lips that would one day do more than pout for ice cream and grin mischievously before he raced into his little boy brand of trouble. Trouble that quite clearly was genetically derived based on the roguish, cut up, and bruised playboy walking next to her.

"I can see that he's most likely mine. And I can do the math." He gentled his tone. "Though it's a shock considering we used protection. I'll run a test to confirm that I'm his father."

Roxy stopped in her tracks next to her vehicle and looked at him. Again, she wanted to punch him in his attractive, sexy face. She'd given up on him and now he wanted to confirm what she'd tried so desperately to tell him years ago? Too little. And way too late. She mentally shook her fist at the sky. Why did this reunion have to occur while she was at her absolute worst and he, no matter how many scrapes and bruises he'd incurred, looked like a gorgeous renegade?

Suddenly her uniform's collar felt like it was constricting the life out of her throat. She stuffed her hormones into a mental never-go-there-again vault. "Run the test. It'll only confirm that your Italian Alpha sperm managed to bust through that so-called protection," she said. "But the results won't change a thing. You've got to do more than contribute sperm to be a considered father material."

A muscle twitched in his jaw, much to her satisfaction. "I'm sure a court will cut me some slack given that I didn't know about the child."

Her pulse kicked into overdrive. "You threatening me?" she asked through icy lips.

"Only if it's warranted." Stefano crossed his arms. "How far I'll take it depends on your willingness to cooperate should it become necessary."

Roxy swallowed hard and willed her racing heart to settle down to a normal clip. "Cooperate?" she asked, her blood boiling. "There's nothing to cooperate about."

Matthew squirmed in her arms and she tightened her grip as she dug out her key fob to unlock the car, opened the backdoor, and carefully situated Matthew into his car seat. Once he was safely strapped in, she kissed the top of his head and ruffled his little boy dark curls. "I've got sole custody. Your name isn't even on the birth certificate. And I plan to keep it that way."

At a little over two years old, Matthew wouldn't understand the conversation, but she desperately wanted to get him away from Stefano and return to the world she'd created after Stefano had broken off all contact with her.

She'd been alone and pregnant. Though she'd tried to find a way to tell Stefano about Matthew afterward via emails to the corporate offices, his staff—more like Gian the jerk—had made it abundantly impossible to relay the information. She'd never known why until today. And even that, the fact that Stefano had believed a background check over and above trusting her, drove a shaft of pain behind her sternum.

"If the test proves I'm his father, I'll pursue custody."

The world tilted beneath her feet, and air whooshed through her ears. "Custody? You'll get custody over my dead body. You haven't been in the picture since *before* I found out I was pregnant. No way will I ever give up my child to you," she said, standing and shielding the still-open passenger door with her body. "You're incapable of caring for

Matthew." Just as he'd been incapable of really loving her.

"I care." A muscle jumped in his handsome stubbled jaw. "About fulfilling my family obligations."

Her pulse rate picked up a notch and anger bubbled through her veins. "I highly doubt that Italy's most notorious playboy wants to be shackled with a child. Unless you have an ulterior motive, which is another reason I won't let you near Matthew." What kind of idiot did he think she was anyway? He'd fooled her once years ago, but now her eyes were wide open.

Long ago she'd spun ridiculous fairy tales about happily-ever-after when he'd murmured Italian words of love and affection during their steamy encounters. Two weeks into their affair, during a romantic dinner, he'd discussed the possibility of bringing Roxy to Italy. That had been followed by the most passionate sexual encounter Roxy had ever experienced.

She'd never forget the following morning when she'd rolled over to embrace Stefano, happy and excited about their future. All she had discovered was a cold, empty space.

A stomach hollowing moment that still made her insides churn today.

"He'll want for nothing if he's mine."

"He wants for nothing now."

Yes, she barely had two dollars to rub together after she paid for her sculpting supplies, Matthew's babysitting costs, and her apartment loft's household bills. But she had no regrets. While there wasn't a whole lot of money, there was always love and laughter. Now she'd make doubly sure that her rights were secured, and no way would she give Stefano any reason to believe her capable of using him for his blasted money. But still, a tiny part of her—the part that recognized the wonder in Stefano's eyes before his need for proof kicked in—wished she could rewind the clock and have a do-over.

But the Momma Bear in her refused to budge an inch for the bastard.

She held the door, turned to look inside the little car and tugged Matthew's car seat strap to double check the locking mechanism. "Okay little buddy, Momma's got to get you to Maura, and then she's going to work."

"This isn't over," Stefano said. "I'll have my lawyers rush everything that's necessary to prove I'm his father and guarantee full custody."

Her breath bottled in her chest. That Stefano questioned his paternity while faced with the reality staring him in his face only made her more certain that she'd never give him a chance to get near Matthew. "He'll never be yours," she said, raising her chin.

Kissing Matthew's little eggshell bump on the right side of his forehead, she cast a glance over her shoulder, taking in Stefano's half-stitched leg. He'd chased her down because of Matthew, not because he had any regrets about leaving her. And that cemented her resolve to fight Stefano every step of the way.

"I won't be cut out of his life if he's mine."

"I'm sure you'll have plenty of legalese to fling at me regarding this situation if you prove paternity." Not that he wouldn't. Adrenaline zipped through her veins and pinpricked in the tips of her fingers, making her hear pound. She didn't know how she'd stop Stefano once he confirmed what she'd known all along, but she had to remain strong for Matthew.

Roxy held Stefano's gleaming blue eyes. "I'm the only parent Matthew's ever known because of your advisors and your idiotic decisions three years ago. That gives me the upper hand in a custody battle. Period."

# Acknowledgments

Critique partners extraordinaire! Carmen Falcone and Pam Mantovani!! Thanks for always having my back, and making me laugh. To my wonderful readers—especially the fabulous Passionettes! Special shout out to Monique Doust, Maria Rose, and Delene Yochum for reading this novella before it went to print. I'm so grateful for your insight. Heidi Scribner and Petra Engle! I'm honored to call you sisters of my heart. Mallory and Chuck! We've had a crazy ride since I sold my first book, but you've stayed the course. I love you both oodles and boodles.

# About Christine Glover

Christine writes tantalizing, sensual, emotional contemporary romances. She enjoys finding the silly in the serious, making wine out of sour grapes, and giving people giggle fits. When she's not writing, you can find her traveling the world, and desperately seeking a corkscrew.

Keep up with Christine's news here: http://eepurl.com/L8Yh5

For more information about Christine and her book releases, go to www.christineglover.com

Facebook:

www.facebook.com/ChristineGloverAuthor/

Twitter: https://twitter.com/cjglover63

# Also by Christine Glover

The Movie Star's Red Hot Holiday Fling: A Sweetbriar Springs' Novella

The Maverick's Red Hot Reunion: Sweetbriar Springs Book 1

The Marine's Red Hot Homecoming: Sweetbriar Springs Book 2

The Tycoon's Red Hot Marriage Merger

The Marriage Ultimatum

Coming Soon!

Hollywood Heartbreakers' Series Spring 2017

Tempting the Heartbreaker: Rafe & Sabrina's Story Book 1

Seducing the Heartbreaker: Jax & Fiona's Story Book 2

Resisting the Heartbreaker: Trevor & Samantha's Story Book 3

72154642R00111

Made in the USA
Columbia, SC
17 June 2017